"You're a terrible actress."

Looking into his eyes, she saw intensity and longing that matched her own. It frightened her. "What do you mean?"

"You don't want to leave any more than I want you to."

In that instant she knew he intended to kiss her. And, surprisingly, she wanted to kiss him back. Her pulse tripled its beat, and her breathing went haywire.

He grasped her arms and tugged her close. Now, the thought of resisting didn't cross her mind. An odd excitement sent a shiver to her bones as his mouth covered hers in a warm, inviting kiss.

Lynne Marshall has been a registered nurse in a large hospital in California for over twenty years. Currently, she is an advice/triage nurse for fifteen internal medicine doctors. She began writing in 2000, and has earned over a dozen contest awards since. She is happily married to a police lieutenant, and has a grown daughter and son. Besides her passion for writing Medical Romance™ stories, she loves travel, reading, and power walks.

Recent titles by the same author:

HER BABY'S SECRET FATHER

HER L.A. KNIGHT

BY
LYNNE MARSHALL

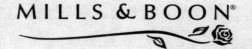

MILLS & BOON®

First published in Great Britain 2007
Paperback edition 2007
Harlequin Mills & Boon Limited,
Eton House, 18-24 Paradise Road, Richmond, Surrey TW9 1SR

© Janet Maarschalk 2007

ISBN-13: 978 0 263 85229 5
ISBN-10:　　 0 263 85229 6

Set in Times Roman 10½ on 12 pt
03-0307-44759

Printed and bound in Spain
by Litografia Rosés, S.A., Barcelona

HER L.A. KNIGHT

To Deanne Avner,
good friend, terrific writer,
and all around peach of a lady!

CHAPTER ONE

"INCOMING," China Seabury announced, hanging up the mobile field-unit phone at the workstation. After five years on the job, she still felt a burst of adrenaline each time someone's life depended on the emergency room.

She shook old memories out of her head, hoping she could remain objective and useful for the patient's sake.

Knowing the ambulance was on its way, and that her window of opportunity to corner Rick Morell would be over in another few seconds, she jogged across the nurses' station to catch up with him. Matching his long-legged strides, she accompanied him down the hallway.

"Hey, Rick," she said, trying not to sound breathless.

Normally she went out of her way to avoid the over-confident, totally full of himself physician's assistant. He looked surprised to find her tagging along.

"What's up, China?"

"You know that fundraiser I've organized next month?"

He lifted a dark brow. "The one you never quit talking about?"

A student nurse appeared out of nowhere, blushing and practically gushing as she handed him a chart. "Can you sign off your orders, please?"

"Sure." After making his scribble, he looked up and smiled at the young nurse. The big blue eyes staring back at him practically melted.

Oh, come on.

The student nurse walked away as if floating on a cloud. Why was it that women threw themselves at his feet? China was hard-pressed to figure it out.

He turned his attention back to her, looking expectant.

"Yeah," China said dryly. "The charity event I never quit talking about, because it's for a good cause."

His masculine gait shifted into a swagger as he got closer to the ambulance entrance. A siren could be heard in the vicinity. He grabbed a bag of normal saline and some IV tubing from the supply cart and, not missing a step, tossed them to her before she could tell him exactly what was on her mind. She caught them deftly.

He cocked his head. "The fundraiser for the teen drivers?"

"Yes. You know exactly what I'm talking about, so quit playing dense."

She juggled the items and stopped abruptly. The thin ER scrubs showcased his broad shoulders and powerful chest. Damn, he'd caught her checking him out. She wished she hadn't noticed, and was damned if she would let him intimidate her. But why couldn't he wear his white coat like all the other PAs?

"I need a master of ceremonies."

His usual confidence changed to downright cocky, a trait she particularly despised, and it almost made her wish she hadn't asked him. How was she going to manage to pull this off without throwing up?

A pleased smile spread across his rugged face. "And I'm your first choice, I presume?"

Oh, yeah, she was definitely going to gag, but she needed his help, and the charity was more important than her pride. She grit her teeth and smiled back. "Would you be interested?"

He rubbed his jaw. "A high profile at the charity auction next month would be great PR."

He kept walking.

She stopped in mid-step. So the rumors she'd heard were true. He planned on applying for the ER supervisor job again.

Vintage Rick with the "what's in it for me?" factor, confirming everything she'd come to know and loathe about him. Why didn't anyone else see him for what he was?

"I'd be glad to, honey." He glanced over his shoulder with a smug grin.

"Rick?"

"Hmm?"

"Don't ever call me 'honey' again."

The emergency room doors blasted open. Two EMTs rolled in a gurney with the motor vehicle accident patient strapped on a backboard and a cervical neck collar in place. They started their report while China and Rick met them.

"Found her car wrapped around a pole on Sunset Boulevard," the first EMT said, pushing through the hall.

"No airway obstruction," said the other, following along. "She's got multiple lacerations and contusions of the face."

China quelled the urge to run screaming out of the ER. It had been ten years—would her post-trauma terrors ever subside?

The patient wailed, and Rick restrained her wrists, lightly wrestling them to her sides.

"We'll take good care of you, miss. You're in good hands." The patient settled at his quiet voice and calm demeanor. Rick helped the men roll the gurney into room three. "The worst is over. Just hang in there."

Oddly, his words helped China control her anxiety. The one positive point about Rick that she would concede was his great bedside manner.

The EMTs transferred the patient to the ER bed, board and all. The patient whimpered with the movement.

"Easy does it. Take a deep breath," Rick said.

China assisted by applying the blood-pressure cuff and monitor leads. She hung the IV bag, which had already been started *en route*, to the hook above the bed, and noted it wasn't infiltrated at the site of insertion. She threaded it into the intravenous infusion machine and set it at 150 cc per hour.

Blood caked in the patient's blond, tri-color high-lighted hair. Her face was a bloody mess, and her nose was obviously broken. China winced at the thought of the pain she must have experienced, flashing back to her own indescribable agony many years before.

"Get stat protocol labs and a portable cross-table lateral cervical spine X-ray," Rick said, stopping abruptly. "Are you OK, China?"

She nodded and swallowed the dry lump in her throat. His gaze lingered, and concern crossed his brow, but not for long. Focusing back on his patient and her needs, he flashed his penlight into her eyes. The patient moaned and blinked. "It's OK," he said. "I'm just looking for glass. You've got a deep cut above your left eyebrow, and another good gash along your right cheek."

He examined her closely and picked a tiny sliver from one of her brows with a tender touch. She looked appreciatively at him.

Back on track, China switched the oxygen cannula from the portable tank to the connection on the wall and did a quick assessment of the patient's body. No obvious sign of broken bones; her chest lifted and dropped evenly with each breath, with no evidence of flail chest. But who knew what internal damage a steering-wheel or an airbag may have caused? Only X-rays would tell for sure.

Once a cervical fracture was ruled out, they'd stabilize her in the ER, remove the protective collar, and send her to Radiology for a full spinal series, along with chest and abdominal X-rays.

The monitor above the bed, besides showing a normal sinus heart rhythm, reported good oxygen saturation from the pulse oximeter she'd slipped on the patient's finger. Maybe the internal damage would be minimal, and she'd be OK, after all.

Taking a deep breath, China rushed out of the room to the phone to order the labs, and paged the X-ray technician. She grabbed the paperwork to enter the patient's identity into the computer and, for the first time, noticed the patient's name. Brianna Cummings.

The teenage actress?

China glanced through the glass wall of the patient's room. She looked so tiny on the ER gurney, nothing like a television star. At her bedside, Rick hovered and listened to her lungs through a stethoscope. A few seconds later, he stuck his head out the door. "Draw up a hundred of Demerol."

She nodded. "Who's got the narcotics keys?"

The charge nurse flung them at her. China caught the keys and hustled to the medicine room.

After China had given the intramuscular shot, Rick caught her on the way out the door. "Do you realize who she is?" he whispered.

China nodded. He followed her back to the medicine room where she double-checked that she'd signed out for the narcotics. He towered over her.

"I'm paging the on-call plastic surgeon to stitch up her face, but I think it's going to take more than skill and a bottomless pit of cash to get her ready for her close-ups again," he said. "Hollywood's a fickle place when it comes to beauty."

She gathered what she needed to clean the patient's facial wounds, somberly shaking her head at the prospect of a young career potentially finished before it had peaked.

"What a waste of a pretty face," he said, and tossed his gloves into the trash.

His impeccable bedside manner had almost fooled her. The man was completely superficial. China came to a halt. "You know, Rick, life isn't all about good looks."

Without missing a beat, as though shooting a basket-ball, he tossed her a package of sterile four by fours. Slam dunk. The slick ER PA only appeared to care about the plight of the young actress.

He started to walk away. "No, China, you're right. Life isn't just about good looks. It's all about appearances."

Fifteen minutes later, Rick slapped the X-ray over the reading lights on the ER wall. He squinted and carefully studied the cervical spine.

His mind drifted to the nurse who had managed to squirm her way into his mind far too often lately. Finally, she'd come to him for something, and all he'd managed to do had been to irritate her.

How many times had he gotten off on the wrong foot with China? He knew what it was like to be an outcast, but preferred not to let on. He also suspected that China's status was self-imposed, which only made her all the more interesting. Though she was completely different from his usual taste in women, he felt drawn to her. Turning thirty had made him re-evaluate his dating game. Maybe it was time to get serious, and she was the type of woman he should pursue.

He chuckled. She couldn't stand him.

The funny thing was, he admired her on many different levels—her dedication, her skill as a nurse, and her passion for her cause. So why did he go out of his way to bother her? Bottom line, he liked giving her a hard time.

Someone needed to lighten her up and teach her that a bright smile always outperformed a grim approach.

He'd learned that the hard way. Just keep smiling. Never let them know how you really feel.

Her tenacity had been the example he'd needed when he'd heard about the ER supervisor job. He'd already been passed over once the previous year, but this time he intended to get hired, and he'd do everything in his power to make sure he got the job.

There was no evidence of a fracture on the X-rays, and for a change he looked forward to being the bearer of good news.

Snapping the X-rays down and replacing them in the folder, he decided that before next month, when he was the master of ceremonies at China's fundraiser, he'd find out everything he could about the topic. And since he couldn't seem to impress China Seabury with ER heroics, he'd try another tack, and this time it would be just cold hard teenage driving statistics.

CHAPTER TWO

One month later.

CHINA HAD TO RUN them over. There was no getting around it. Zooming down the 405 Freeway in Los Angeles, closed in on both sides by cars traveling no less than seventy-five miles an hour, the runaway balloons couldn't be avoided.

Her hands tightened on the wheel. Fear crushed through her chest. What if she swerved? She might sideswipe another car. Oh, God, she didn't want to do that.

She had no choice but to hit and run. Fighting the urge to close her eyes, she kept her foot on the gas and plowed full speed ahead.

It wasn't a clean drive-over. No. The air flow from the cars on each outside lane whipped up and off the road, and she hit the balloons at an angle, a cluster of deflating party balloons, complete with bright ribbons, and instead of popping, they hooked onto her front bumper.

The black and silver, over-the-hill, thick-skinned-helium balloons meant for someone else flopped and thumped against her windshield, blocking her vision. They were a sad commentary on how her big day had been going.

Her heart rapped against her chest. The last thing she needed was to have an accident on her way to a fund-raiser for safe driving.

China slowed down a bit and, reaching between her seat and the inside of the car door, adjusted the bucket seat position. Maybe then she could see around the balloons until she had a chance to exit the freeway.

Nothing changed, at least not inside the car. Having pulled the wrong lever, the trunk of her car flew open. Now not only was her front vision impaired, but the view out the back was, too.

She gripped the steering-wheel tighter and let up a little more on the accelerator. She didn't want to die on her twenty-seventh birthday.

Above the flapping trunk, a red light flashed in her eyes.

She shook her head. Hell.

Strangely relieved, she took her first breath, not having been aware she'd been holding it. Traffic parted in her path. She steered the car to the shoulder of the road and waited for the highway patrol officer to approach. Hopefully, he'd offer a sympathetic ear.

After fishing out her car registration from the glove compartment, China checked her rear-view mirror. She caught a glimpse of herself, once again shocked at how short her bangs were, and rolled her eyes.

How had she let her hairdresser talk her into it? Not once in her life had she ever aspired to look like Cleopatra. Yet here she was, sitting on the side of the

405 Freeway, about to get a moving violation ticket while dressed in a black velvet toga-style dress, looking like the old asp-handling seductress herself.

Sheesh.

She couldn't think of one single day in her life that sucked worse than today.

Memory wouldn't let the lie take hold. No, that wasn't true. Even with her lousy hairdo, the half-dead balloons stuck on her car, the imminent ticket, and yet another birthday without a date, today hadn't come close to the worst day of her life ten years earlier.

In her mind's eye, she saw the twisted metal, heard the cacophony of screams and horns, and felt the molten daggers of pain, on the day that had changed her for ever.

Shaking off the recurring nightmarish memory, China put the balloon incident into perspective.

It didn't even come close.

She waited for the highway patrolman to finish his paperwork.

Thankful to be alive, she watched cars whiz past. The officer walked to the front of her automobile, unhooked the droopy balloons, held them like a sad bouquet, and strolled toward her window.

Wincing with embarrassment, she held out hope he'd see her side of the story.

The reticent officer took the license and registration she handed him through the window, glanced at them and, with a deadpan face, handed her the deflating balloons and said, "Happy Birthday, Ms. Seabury."

Grateful for the kindness of the amused-looking highway patrol officer who hadn't given her a ticket,

China only arrived fifteen minutes late for the charity dinner. She parked her car in the reserved spot, something she'd earned for working endless hours putting the whole event together. Gathering her skirt, she ran like a girlie-girl in fancy high-heeled shoes toward the entrance.

She flung the auditorium doors wide to expose a noisy, chattering crowd. The open bar and general festivities had already begun at the hundred-dollar-a-plate event.

Pleased with the turnout, she slowed down at the sight. All the tables were filled. Several hundred balloons were corralled in a net on the ceiling, waiting to be released when the charity grand total was announced later. Excitement buzzed in the air.

Nurses loved any excuse to wear something other than scrubs or starchy white uniforms, and they'd showed up in full party regalia tonight.

China savored the moment. She'd worked tirelessly on her days off to make this dream happen. Week after week, working forty hours on the evening shift in the Mercy Hospital emergency room, the point had been driven home: teenagers were careless drivers, causing the majority of accidents and ER visits. Statistics didn't lie. She knew the facts firsthand. Her scars would never let her forget it.

"China." She recognized her sister Sierra's voice and looked beyond a vast sea of sparkling white tablecloths adorned with colorful centerpieces. A fellow ER RN, Sierra sat close to the stage. "Psst. Over here."

Snaking her way through the large round tables, China tripped on a chair. Her weak ankle twisted and she slid off her shoe, but she caught herself before she fell on her face.

Feeling like a klutz and thankful for the dimness, she scrambled to retrieve her strappy-heeled sandal. She made her way to her sister's table in deep blush.

"Where the heck have you been?" Sierra whispered.

"You don't want to know. Trust me."

"I was freaking out that you'd had an accident or something."

"I forgot my cellphone. Sorry I couldn't call." She smiled and patted her older sister reassuringly on the arm. "I'm fine. You look nice."

Sierra wore a flashy scoop-necked dress with lots of bobbles and dangly feathers, reminding China of her mother. Her wild mane of auburn hair competed with the metallic copper-colored outfit, but somehow, on her, it worked.

"What happened to your hair?" Sierra screwed up her face, zeroing in on China's straight black tresses. "Your bangs don't even cover your scar."

Feeling suddenly more self-conscious, China tugged on them, as if they might grow on the spot. "It was Rigoberto's idea of the latest fashion trend. Do I look like a total fool?"

Sierra's face softened. Smile lines crinkled around her dark green eyes. "Hardly. I've heard the Cleopatra look is coming back." She made a sideways V with her fingers and scooped them across her eyes. "But where's your eye make-up?"

China moaned, thinking how ridiculous she must look.

They'd been told they had the same eyes, though

they were only half-sisters, same mom, different dads. Their exotic names reflected the taste of their green-eyed, hippy, free-spirit mom. Marriage had never been her thing, leaving the siblings fatherless, and to bond under challenging circumstances. But bond they had, and were fiercely protective of each other.

Sierra pouted. "Aw, come on, you know I'm teasing." She leaned one way, moved her head from side to side, then leaned the other direction and did the same, while checking her out. "I think I like it."

"Well, whew, I'm all better now," China said. She screwed up her lips and looked upward, as if she might be able to see her own bangs. Her eyes crossed.

A light flashed.

Sierra, doing double duty as the hospital underground newsletter editor, had taken a picture. "Happy birthday!"

"I'm going to kill you." China lunged at her.

Sierra whisked her camera safely away and slipped it inside her purse. "Too late," she said.

The lights came up in the room, distracting China momentarily.

"You'll pay for this, Ms. Paparazzi," she said, turning her attention to the stage.

"Welcome. It's great to see everyone here tonight. I'm Rick Morell, and I'll be your host."

China shook her head, thinking of what she'd managed to do for the love of her charity. The thought of a humiliating picture in the newsletter was a small price to pay. And besides, her mother and Sierra were always telling her not to be so uptight.

Well, she'd lightened up enough to go out of her way

to ask Mercy Hospital's very own snake charmer to be master of ceremonies. Wasn't that something?

She couldn't figure out why women went gaga around him. Good looks weren't everything.

It was no surprise that he'd taken her up on the offer to MC. The guy loved attention, especially female attention. He used the old heroics routine on a daily basis in the ER, always finding some way to impress the younger nurses. He wouldn't miss an opportunity to strut his stuff in front of a room filled with women. It might drum up a few more dates.

He looked slick in a three-quarter-length, Western-cut black tuxedo with silver-tipped bola tie. His thick brown hair touched the collar, and pointy cowboy dress boots completed the picture of rough and rugged masculinity.

His lopsided smile was another story, pure charm all the way. Perhaps it was the terrific cheekbones and strong jaw. Or maybe it was the cleft in his chin, but she didn't want to think about it.

China refused to be drawn in by the alluring sparkle in his dark eyes. Some might call him sexy. Not her. She preferred something subtler than glitz and charm, and deeper than stylishly hot. And besides, he was out of her league, and she never intended to get involved with anyone again. Who needed to be chewed up and spit out more than once?

But looking around the room, everyone else, including her married sister, seemed to have a different idea about what was sexy. Having now taken the digital camera back out of her purse, Sierra snapped his picture.

China rolled her eyes when he smiled on cue.

Get over yourself, buddy.

Life was all about appearances, hadn't he said that? Was she the only one in the room that had him nailed as a phony?

She scanned the crowd again. Every female, and even a few men, sat staring at the stage, enthralled.

Apparently she was the only one.

"He's what I'd call a ten," Sierra whispered.

"Yeah, a ten on a jerk scale." China crossed her arms, daring him to impress her.

Rick flashed another smile. "As you know, we're here tonight for a worthy cause: to help teens realize there is more to driving than getting a license. Each year approximately 5,000 teenagers lose their lives behind the wheel of a car in the United States. Almost 31,000 people have died in the last decade due to teenage crashes. Sixteen- and seventeen-year-olds have the highest crash rate per mile of any age group. The crash rate increases five times over when a teenager drives unsupervised with three other teen passengers. Countless innocent people's lives are ruined because of irresponsible young drivers."

He paused and surveyed the audience with a dramatic gaze.

"Recently I'm sure you all read about the Brianna Cummings driving accident. I asked her permission to mention it tonight. Because of careless driving she almost didn't make it to her nineteenth birthday. Now a month later, she's had to have her nose fixed, and will have to undergo several other operations in the future to diminish her facial scars. I'm sure one day she'll again be as beautiful as the heroine we all know from the hit television show, *The Undead,* but it will be a long process. The only bright spot in her story is she didn't kill or injure anyone else."

The spirited crowd grew somber. Throats cleared, random coughs accentuated the quiet.

"Teenagers may feel invincible behind the wheel, but a lifetime of guilt and consequences is a tough pill to swallow at any age when you've taken someone else's life away."

China's gut churned. She hadn't given him that bit to say, he must have done his own research. And damn if he hadn't hit the nail on the head, too. But he'd forgotten to add the part about spending the rest of your life trying to make up for it.

She lifted a brow; he'd charmed the audience then struck like a snake with statistics and the ugly face of reality.

He lightened the moment with a corny medical joke. "But moving on, I have a question for you. How many nurses does it take to screw in a light bulb? One. And she'll be glad to tell everyone else on the ward exactly how to do it, too."

China applauded along with the receptive audience sprinkled with a boo here and there. She eased back in her chair, relaxing for the first time since she'd left home. She'd made the right choice in Rick.

"But I think you should hear more about why we're here tonight from our very own crusading, ER nurse *extraordinaire*, China Seabury."

What? She stopped in mid-clap. No!

"Come on up." Rick motioned for her to join him. Didn't he know about her stage fright?

How could he? They'd hardly ever spoken more than five words to each other.

Blood drained from her face and pooled in her stomach. She felt queasy. Before her accident, she had been captain of her debate team, but ever since that day she'd lost all the confidence she'd ever had for public speaking.

Sierra patted her arm and helped her stand up. The room went silent, and China slowly realized they were waiting for her to join Rick on the stage.

Sheer willpower moved her feet. Her hands trembled and she prayed she wouldn't catch her long skirt on a chair. She knew her subject as well as her own name, yet right this second she wasn't even sure of that.

China made it up the steps, but her mouth went drier than the desert when Rick pushed the microphone her way. Stunned, her eyes widened. He must have noticed her distress. His large hand guided her to the podium, and she caught a glint of concern in his gaze. She looked helplessly at him and her mind went blank.

He licked his lips and retrieved the microphone. Clearing his throat, he smiled broadly at China, then at the crowd.

"I guess I've surprised China." Looking sympathetically at her and covering the microphone with his hand, he whispered, "I didn't mean to put you on the spot. I assumed you'd want to speak tonight."

Frozen in place, she couldn't get her mouth to work. A whirling sound started in her ears. She willed herself not to faint.

He tightened his grip on her arm, and slipped his

hand around her waist. "Don't worry, I've got you," he murmured.

He held the mike for her. She moistened her lips, gulped, and forced a smile. "Um, I want to…th-thank all of you for coming tonight. You've helped make this a b-big success. But if you da-don't mind, I'll um turn the evening over to Rick."

A swell of applause helped her realize she'd made another good decision. Relief rushed over her as blood returned to her face. She'd survived. Steadying her legs, she left the stage with as much dignity as she could conjure up. Thank God she didn't trip on her way down.

Angry that he'd pulled a fast one on her, and wanting nothing more than to flee the building, she forced her head high. She walked placidly back to her table, doing her best not to limp, and sat.

Rick watched China leave the stage. Her sleek black hair hung model-straight to her narrow shoulders with a new and stylish interpretation of bangs. The word "chic" came to mind. It looked so much better than the usual severe French twist she wore at work.

He'd never noticed the pale white half-moon-shaped scar above her brow before. Instead of distracting from her appeal, it only added to her intrigue. This new glamorous look was a side of China he'd never seen before. Though he had fantasized about the possibility on several occasions.

Normally, she had a creamy complexion, but tonight she'd gone ivory white, making her red lips even more inviting. Her jade-green eyes turned naturally upward, and they'd flashed a look of panic at him.

Truth be told, he'd wanted her to faint, so he could catch her.

So little Miss Competent had a vulnerable side.

And the beauty of it all was she didn't have a clue how deeply she affected him. Other guys at work had called her uptight and average-looking, but he thought they were nuts. Sure, she was wired tight, but he'd seen her smile a few times. Couldn't they see her for what she was, serious and devoted to her job? Being the exact opposite of his usual lady friends, China fascinated him. Maybe it was time for his taste in women to mature. And maybe China was just the ticket.

Something deep and dark lurked behind those striking green eyes. And if he played his cards right, he'd get the chance to find out what it was.

Anchoring her to his hip at the podium had given him a rush when he'd caught the scent of exotic herbs with a touch of vanilla. For such a petite woman she'd felt deceptively substantial under his grasp. He'd like nothing more than to explore the rest of China, but he had a job to do.

He tore his gaze away from her and flashed his most dashing smile at the audience. "I guess you're stuck with me."

Whoops and whistles made him smile even broader. No need for the usual bravado. With little effort he had the audience right where he wanted them, eating out of his hand.

Willing them to remember that he wanted to be Mercy Hospital's next emergency room supervisor. He'd filled out his application for the soon-to-be-posted job just that morning.

His gaze roamed the room and he found his father, the king of conditional love, in the crowd. At the sight of his stone-cold stare, Rick's moment of glory dissolved into self-doubt.

China seemed to be the moment's golden girl, with her crusade for teenage drivers bringing Mercy Hospital loads of publicity and his father's glowing seal of approval. She deserved every bit of it. Though he hoped his father's opinion of China wouldn't go down once he discovered she was dating his slacker son, because he had every intention of asking her out.

Once China sat back down and drained half of the water in her glass, she felt better.

Rick spoke in the background, but she couldn't focus on his words. Everyone laughed at another dumb nurse joke.

Sierra patted her on the shoulder. "Great job, sis."

China glared. "I'm going to kill him for doing that to me."

"Isn't that overreacting just a tad?"

"Not the way I feel right now, it isn't."

"How was he supposed to know about your phobia about public speaking?"

China tossed her head. Sierra was right, but she was damned if she'd cut him any slack. She glanced around the table at five other nurses, all grinning and staring at the stage. The chair next to her remained empty.

Rick finished his speech by entreating everyone to eat and enjoy, and to be sure to open their wallets for the basket auction later.

He swaggered off the stage and down the steps, strolling toward her table.

China groaned and impaled her sister with another life-threatening stare. Ever the matchmaker, Sierra smiled and raised her eyebrows a couple of times. "I saved him a seat."

Instead of sitting, Rick pulled out the vacant chair, turned it around, and swung his leg over as if mounting a horse, using the back as an armrest.

"So how are all of you lovely ladies doing tonight?" He glanced around the table, settling his eyes on China.

The excited group of nurses obliged him by speaking over each other in response. China tried her best to sink back into oblivion. Raising money for charity really was a sacrifice.

"We did good, no?" He smiled directly at her.

"Yeah, yeah, rub it in," she said.

He lifted China's wrist, felt her pulse and said, "You'll live. A little stage fright is good for you."

The waiter approached with their meals. China slipped her hand free, aggravated by the subtle chills running up her arm, and Rick turned his seat back around to the table.

While thinking horrible thoughts about how she'd like to crown him for making her go on stage, China forced on her diplomatic fundraising hat. "Well, I can't thank you enough for helping out tonight, Rick. You certainly lived up to your reputation as Mr. Personality." She snapped out her napkin a little more dramatically than necessary, and placed it across her lap.

"Not a problem, China. I'm always glad to be of service." He winked.

Another surge of anger had China biting the inside of her mouth. How dare he flirt with her?

Sierra spoke up. "Too bad we couldn't auction you off as a date tonight. We'd have raised a few thousand more dollars."

China kneed her sister under the table.

"Ouch."

"I think that's a little politically incorrect these days, don't you?" China said.

"Hey," Rick said. "Not if it's all in good fun for the right cause. Heck, I'd have been willing."

Sierra pursed her lips and gave China an I-told-you-so gaze.

"I'm sure you would have," China said.

She shook her head and glanced up in time to see the head of internal medicine approach their table. And for the first time she noticed Rick's sunny disposition fade. His charming smile hardened to a straight line. His brown eyes grew cautious and dark.

Dr. Morell, Rick's father, extended his hand to China, gave a limp shake, and glanced around the table. He nodded at his son as though he were a mere acquaintance. Rick tipped his head the slightest bit in response.

China realized how much they resembled each other, and had to admit the older man was still good-looking.

"I wanted to compliment you on the exceptional turnout tonight. I trust the funds will be put to good use?" he said.

"Oh, yes. I've been working with the police and fire departments on a program for the local high schools about responsible driving. I've even got a surprise guest lined up."

"Well, keep up the good work on behalf of Mercy Hospital."

He left abruptly without acknowledging his son's contribution toward the evening's success. A nagging age-old need to make right all the injustices in the world had China speaking before she'd thoroughly thought things through.

"Rick, I am terribly afraid of speaking in public. But I'm sure you realized that on the stage. I'm a behind-the-scenes kind of girl. And, well...I don't know how I can ever thank you enough for helping me out tonight."

Having recovered from his father's snub, the old snake-charmer spark returned to Rick's eyes. His smile brightened. "I can think of a few ways."

She blushed and turned to her sister to change the subject, but he spoke before she had a chance.

"Why don't you repay me by going out with me?" He quickly glanced down at his plate and back up. "Let me buy you dinner."

"Hey, that's a great idea. She'll take it," Sierra accepted quickly on China's behalf.

China kicked her sister's foot and watched Sierra wither under the death look she threw her. But having finished a glass of wine, Sierra didn't know when to keep quiet.

"It's been a long time since you've had an evening out, China. There's more to life than charity fundraising, meetings, and work. I just thought maybe you and Rick would enjoy each other's company. He's always good for a laugh in the ER so he's probably a real kick on a date. Right, Rick?"

"You know I am."

Seeing red with a combination of anger and embarrassment, China glowered at her sister, then pretended to smile for Rick. He turned on his lopsided grin and raised his brows, looking far more charming than China cared to admit.

"Just dinner." He placed his wide palm over his heart. "I promise."

China shook her head.

"Look," he said, taking out his checkbook, "I'll make a $500 donation tonight for the honor of taking you out. It's for a good cause. What do you say?"

Once again speechless, China looked at her traitorous sister.

"Yes," Sierra said. "She says yes."

CHAPTER THREE

"SMILE for me," China coaxed her fifty-something patient, the following Monday afternoon. He gave a one-sided, sagging smile. "Now lift your eyebrows." Only one shot up. "Can you close your eyes tightly?" It looked more like a single-eyed wink.

The man, a schoolteacher, had been admitted to the ER fearing he'd had a stroke when he'd woken up with half of his face paralyzed.

"How am I going to teach like this?"

His left cheek drooped and his eye teared. The medical history China had taken revealed that no injury had occurred, and no disease process played into the condition. His blood pressure was normal, his handgrip was even bilaterally, and he had full use of his left extremities. Her biggest concern was that he might develop permanent nerve damage from what she suspected to be Bell's palsy.

"If it's any consolation, I can understand everything you're saying," she said. "And I'm sure your students will, too. But if you feel uncomfortable I'm sure you can get a substitute teacher for a few days. "

Rick strolled by the exam room.

She zipped outside to catch him. "Hey, Rick?"

He turned expectantly, holding a staple gun, and gave a pleased grin. "Ah, our date. Yes, we need to make plans."

She sighed and rolled her eyes. "No. As a matter of fact, I was looking for Dr. Weinstein. Have you seen him?"

He shook his head.

She gestured toward the patient exam room. "Hey, since nurses aren't supposed to diagnose and physicians' assistants can, and the doctor is tied up with another patient, I need you to examine this guy. I think it's Bell's palsy. He'll probably need a script for prednisone, but Dr. Weinstein can write that when we run everything by him." She motioned for him to follow her.

"I'd love to, China, but first I've got to staple up a head wound."

"Oh. OK."

"Give me ten minutes, and if you haven't found Dr. Weinstein by then, I'll be right with you."

A half-hour later, with prescription in hand for steroid therapy and a follow-up appointment with his personal physician, and following a crash course from Rick on eye care and muscle exercises to prevent permanent damage, the teacher was discharged and escorted out of the ER.

China smiled and handed him his insurance form, reassuring him that he'd have a good chance of spontaneously recovering from Bell's palsy. Only time would tell for sure how long it could take.

Though he'd been unexpectedly put off work, leaving his school in limbo, she knew substitute teachers could replace him over the next month or six weeks. Being a teacher in the public school system, he had excellent medical benefits and, if necessary, he'd get disability pay.

She turned to see which patient was next; instead, she found Rick. He stood resolute, broad shoulders filling out his blue scrub top, arms folded, legs in a wide stance. With swept-back nut-brown hair and a determined stare, he looked dashing, and it irked China to no end that she'd noticed.

"It's pretty quiet. Why don't you take your dinner break with me in, say…" he glanced at his watch "…right now?"

China frantically searched for a reason to get out of it, but there wasn't even one new patient chart lined up in the cubicles by the triage nurse's station. A rare occurrence in the ER. China feared she'd been dragged into a subversive plot master minded by her evil sister, whom she still hadn't forgiven. She nervously scanned the half-empty ER and found Sierra, who waved and smiled at her from across the clinic with a clipboard in her hand.

China launched a couple of angry missiles at her with a quick squint. Sierra stuck out her tongue. Fighting the desire to return the favor, she recovered and instead made a diffident smile for Rick.

"Sure." China shrugged it off. May as well get it over with. "Dinner right now, why not?"

"Well, in that case, let's go." He wrapped his strong hand around her arm and led her through the ER door, calling over his shoulder on the way out, "We're on break."

* * *

China nibbled at her hospital cafeteria salad, mostly moving it around on her plate. Her vegetable soup had gotten cold. Despite her desire to find Rick otherwise, she discovered his casual banter to be light-hearted, witty and, yes, much to her dismay, fun.

"So this psych patient says to me, 'I'm being stalked by my next-door neighbor, Mr. Boots. Everywhere I turn he's there—in my living room, on the hood of my car, under my bed.' I'm thinking to myself this guy's either really got a problem or he's totally paranoid and needs to get back on his meds, quick." He scratched his long, straight nose and smothered a smile. "When I asked him to describe the neighbor to me, I finally figured out he was talking about a cat." Rick grinned and shoveled some meatloaf into his mouth.

China laughed, and let go of another layer of tension. OK, so he knew how to entertain. But he still had all the markings of a cad. Several nurses in the cafeteria had gone out of their way to get his attention. She'd suspected that he'd probably dated most of them but, in his favor, he ignored them, concentrating solely on her.

A sense of dread about how much gossip she'd have to endure for being seen with Rickk made her tense up again. The other nurses were probably wondering what in the heck he was doing with plain old China.

Not that she wasn't wondering the same thing.

Trying to keep the conversation going, she asked, "Have they interviewed you for the ER supervisor job yet?"

He shook his head.

"Don't they usually reserve it for a nurse practitioner?"

"It's about time they changed that, don't you think, China?"

He had a point. She weighed the issue. PA? Or RNP? Both required advanced degrees. One trained by nurses and the other trained by doctors. The best person should get the job. She lifted a noncommittal shoulder. "I guess the suits will decide."

"Undoubtedly."

"So how come you didn't want to become a doctor, like your father?"

He raised an eyebrow. "Let me ask you this, have you ever wanted to be like your mother?"

Cass Seabury's cherubic face and Rubensesque shape came to mind. Her mother, the rich trust-fund child, spoiled teen, and unconventional adult who'd lived life exactly the way she'd wanted. A woman who'd never looked back, regardless of the damage she'd done. Her mother was one of a kind.

"Oh, hell no." China took a bite of her sourdough roll, shivering at the thought of being anything like her mother. No, unlike her mom, she chose to hold her regrets close to her heart, like dear old friends that she never wanted to let go. Old friends she could torture herself with whenever guilt took hold. And in life, according to China, guilt was abundant.

He nodded. "You see? I rest my case."

Their knees touched under the table. China quickly moved hers, but not before an electric message snaked up her leg. She furrowed her brows and looked at Rick. The moment hadn't been lost on him either.

The hint of a smile crossed his lips before he continued talking. "I wanted to see the world and have some excitement, instead of burying my nose in text-books for ten years."

"You were in the services, right?"

"Yep. I went into the army right out of high school and became a medic. I got most of my clinical training in the field, though."

Rick was well respected for his knowledge of trauma medicine. It made sense that he'd learned what he knew on the front line.

"And I gotta admit it was kind of sweet to join up and stick it to my father at the same time." His signature mischievous grin appeared. "Instead of packing up for a dorm room the year after my mother died, I got shipped off to barracks. By choice."

China had noticed a strained silence between father and son any time they were in the same vicinity, and had wondered why. Rick always seemed cautious around Dr. Morell. And Dr. Morell seemed flat out dismissive of Rick. Maybe Rick's choice of the army over college explained their behavior toward each other.

Their beepers went off simultaneously. China checked hers, already knowing who it was. With no need to explain to each other where they were headed, they rushed a couple more bites of dinner into their mouths, grabbed their cafeteria trays and headed for the ER.

Nurses and doctors bustled around the drab, institution-green linoleum floors, darting in and out of several glass cubicles encased by pale gray walls. An attempt to brighten up the place with prints of seascapes had fallen flat. The familiar antiseptic odor made its presence known, along with a few demanding patients calling out from the numbered rooms that circled the central nurses' station.

Within only thirty minutes the ER had changed from being quiet and half-empty to filled to capacity with patients, loud banter, and an occasional groan. And from the looks of the triage station, there were more people waiting.

Upon their arrival, the charge nurse pointed in the direction they were needed. Two firemen were in the midst of transferring a young man from a gurney to an ER bed. The kid let out an pain-filled yell when they lifted and moved him on the count of three.

Rick stepped up to the bedside, eyes scanning the patient. "Hey, champ. What's up?"

The teenager groaned.

"Don't worry. We're gonna take good care of you." He placed his big hand on the patient's thigh, and though it looked as if he was just being friendly China knew he was starting his initial assessment.

China checked and retaped the IV that had been started in the field, and picked up the chart and read his name and age. The boy was only eighteen. She hooked him up to the blood-pressure machine on the unaffected arm, and pushed the button.

"Chad fell off the roof, helping his dad clean the gutters after school," the first fireman said. "No spinal damage, but his shoulder is probably shattered."

"How far did he fall? Did he hit anything on the way down?" Rick asked, continuing to assess his patient.

The other fireman spoke up. "About eighteen or so feet. Straight fall. Nothing in between." A saddened look appeared on his big swarthy face. "He's the quarterback at Valley View High School."

China wanted to get the poor kid some immediate relief from his pain. "Are you allergic to any medicine?"

The kid grimaced and shook his head. She wrote down his elevated blood-pressure reading, noting it was probably due to his discomfort. She'd watch for signs of shock once his adrenaline rush wore off.

"Draw up 75 milligrams of Demerol," Rick instructed.

"Write it down," she said, handing him the green doctor's orders, knowing she'd have to get it cosigned later by the ER doctor that Rick was assigned to. She headed for the med room for some Demerol, stopping only long enough to call the X-ray tech for a portable X-ray of the shoulder.

The firemen had left, the anxious parents had arrived, and Rick examined his patient's shoulder. He'd had to use bandage scissors to remove Chad's shirt rather than make him move when he knew lifting even one millimeter would hurt like hell. Bruised and swollen, the shoulder was oddly shaped, and the humerus was most likely fractured. The clavicle looked broken, too. Suspicious that more than a simple shoulder dislocation was the culprit, he continued examining the patient and palpated his chest, sternum, ribs, liver and abdomen for damage. So far, things had checked out all right.

The mother whimpered in the background. The father wrapped his arm around her and drew her close. Chad bit his lower lip and said, "I'll be OK, Ma." Tears brimmed in his eyes.

Rick's heart wrenched at the sight, but he didn't let on. His mother had died when he'd been a teenager, and he still missed her dearly. As for him and his father, well, there was no love lost there. Mom had had cancer and Dad had withdrawn. Enough said.

"Can you move your fingers?" He began his neurological assessment. The teenager wiggled them cautiously, moaning with the effort. Rick touched Chad's fingertips with a pin. "Can you feel this?"

He nodded.

The nail beds on the affected side were a bit dusky, but when he pressed them, they blanched and the capillaries quickly refilled with pink blood. If his prediction was right, there was no nerve or deep vessel damage and his shoulder had taken the brunt of the fall.

He lifted his eyebrows. If Chad had landed a couple centimeters one way or the other, he could have broken his neck and wound up paralyzed or, worse yet, dead. Worst-case scenario, a pulverized shoulder joint could be wired together and dealt with in this day and age of titanium and joint replacements if need be.

Regardless of what the X-rays revealed, how would he explain to an eighteen-year-old quarterback that he wouldn't be throwing a football the rest of the season?

China whisked into the cubicle like a fresh healing breeze, and smiled at the teenager.

"Relief," she said, displaying the filled syringe. "I'm going to use your thigh so you won't have to roll onto your side."

"Thanks," Chad said, apprehension disappearing from his eyes.

Rick admired China's easygoing manner with

patients. Her calm attitude helped relieve her patients'
worst fears, even if only for a minute or two. He also
suspected that Chad, though wrung out with pain,
noticed how sexy she was. And a nurturing woman
could always make any situation better.

Rather than dealing with his belt and jeans, and
wanting the medicine to affect his patient a lot quicker,
Rick made a suggestion. "Why don't you titrate the
Demerol IV push?"

Procedural sedation in the ER was still a sticky
subject with hospital administration, unless a doctor
was at the bedside, but his patient's comfort came first.
And theoretically there were several doctors nearby. He
nodded to China to go ahead.

She nodded back and worked quickly to connect
Chad to the heart monitor for added observation, and
finished by placing an oxygen saturation meter on the
nail bed of his finger. Then she switched the long needle
for an IV tubing friendly lever-lock plastic one, and
swabbed the rubber port with alcohol. She crimped the
tubing and expertly delivered 25 mg of Demerol into
the IV over the next minute, followed by another 25 mg
over another minute or so. When Chad showed no signs
of being nauseated and started to look sedated, she
glanced at Rick. He nodded to indicate that 50 mg IV
of the painkiller was enough. He watched her waste the
remaining 25 mg of Demerol then dispose of the needle
in the sharps container. She checked the IV machine,
and looked satisfied that all was well.

A normal sinus rate and rhythm on the monitor once
again proved the resilient powers of youth.

The X-ray technician appeared like a bumper car

with his noisy, portable motor operated-machine,
forcing his way into the room. Now was as good a time
as any to clear out.

Rick escorted the parents toward the waiting room
and asked the ward clerk to order a routine pre-op lab
panel. If the X-ray revealed what he suspected, a shattered joint head and a fractured humerus, Rick might
have to notify the on-call orthopedic surgeon for emergency surgery. Hopefully, that wouldn't be necessary,
it would be better to stabilize Chad, drug him up and
make him comfortable for the night. A well-rested
surgeon was imperative, too. Rather than adding on a
case after a long day, he'd wait for the X-ray results,
then suggest they wait until bright and early the next
morning for surgery.

If it turned out to be a mere shoulder dislocation,
though, he'd reduce the joint a.s.a.p. to prevent permanent nerve or circulation damage. Either way, the
surgeon promised to come by and examine the patient
after the X-rays were in. They'd go from there.

Rick planned to stabilize the joint with a shoulder
immobilizer, keeping the arm flush to Chad's chest.
The less movement, the less pain the patient would
feel, until morning when he'd get sent to surgery for
open reduction and internal fixation. In the meantime,
Rick would send him to the holding area.

His eyes wandered across the clinic and found
China, pert and concentrating on making chart entries.
Her shiny ink-colored hair was pulled tightly back into
the usual French twist, except for her short fringe of
bangs. She wore a white scrub top and string-tied pants,
and clogs with thick, colorful athletic socks, yet she still

managed to look sexy. If he squinted, he could almost
see the outline of French-cut panties through her scrubs.
Too bad she didn't treat him like a patient. He'd appreciate some of her easygoing bedside manner instead of
the nurse from hell routine.

He'd made some progress during their break. After
all, he'd actually made her laugh. And who knew what
he could accomplish with a little more time?

Regrettably turning from the pleasant thought of
China with a fresh-from-making-love blush, he realized
he hadn't made arrangements with her for their purchased date yet. Never one to miss an opportunity, he
walked across the ER and quietly approached her.

She must have felt his presence before he spoke. Her
eyes drifted upward, all business when she looked at
him. He'd have to do something about that, but not right
now.

After thorough physical examination, he knew in
his gut the kid's shoulder was pummeled beyond repair.
Time and X-ray results would prove it one way or the
other. Still, he couldn't stop himself from using an age-
old survival technique, making light of life in the ER.

"It's a shame that kid's college scholarship is going
down the gutter," he said. "Literally."

She looked thoughtful and distant when she nodded
her head. "You're awfully quick to write people off,
aren't you?"

"I'm just speaking the truth."

"You know with physical therapy and a lot of hard
work, he may get 100 per cent range of motion back
someday."

"Not before he graduates high school." Rick rubbed

his face with his hand and wished he could tap into his optimistic side once in a while. He glanced across at the boy's persistent parents who'd come back into the ER and were waiting patiently outside the room for the X-ray technician to leave. "Let's be honest, the odds of his throwing another football this season are nil, unless he's ambidextrous."

"Until we get the X-rays back we can't be sure of the full extent of his injury." She looked pleased with herself, like he hadn't already considered that part of the equation.

"Let's hope."

She lifted her chin. "May I ask whatever happened to your compassion gene?"

"I've got plenty of compassion. Well, the *passion* part anyway." He tried his charming-to-a-fault look, the one that usually got a smile out of a woman. Instead, it fell on uninterested, though exotic, eyes. Rising to the challenge, he grinned.

"Listen," he said. "I didn't get a chance to talk about our date over dinner."

She stiffened and went looking for something under a stack of papers. "You don't have to take me out, Rick. Besides, we just had dinner, and you said 'just dinner'. Remember? So, as far as I'm concerned, if you want to reimburse me, we're set."

A few wisps of dark hair had escaped her severe hairdo. They framed her face and played with her milky white neck. He had a sudden urge to do the same, but with his fingertips. Instead, he cleared his throat.

"Oh, no, you don't. You're not getting off the hook that easily. Not for a mere five bucks in a hospital cafeteria."

For the first time in the conversation she glanced at him. "It's just that I think my sister put you on the spot." Her earnest eyes looked like emeralds.

"Not at all. If anyone's on the spot it's you, and guess what? I don't care." He grinned even wider. "How about this weekend?"

She shook her head. "We're both scheduled to work."

Thinking fast, he jumped back in. "I've got Friday night off—how about you?"

She hesitated, and glanced toward the posted ER work schedule hanging on a clipboard on the wall outside the medication room.

Before she had a chance to make any changes, he strode across the floor and yanked it from its hook. She rushed behind him, making quick clog sounds, as if she thought she could beat him to it.

He whisked it up and above her head. "Oh, no you don't." He held it playfully at a distance and searched for the information he hoped would clinch the deal. Damn. She was scheduled to work Friday, and had Thursday off.

A pleased grin stretched across her full red-tinted lips when she realized the work schedule was in her favor. Sierra walked up behind her.

"Hey, China, I can switch my Friday with your Thursday so you can go out with Rick." She carried a thoracentesis tray and only stopped long enough to foil China's plans for reneging on going out with him.

China's grin disappeared and her mouth dropped open.

"Well there you go, honey. Looks like it was meant to be."

"What'd I tell you about comparing me to food?" China shook her head.

"You know, a guy could get an inferiority complex seeing your attitude about a date with me." He pretended to be hurt, but enjoyed the whole set-up. He couldn't have paid Sierra enough for her perfect timing.

China took her time answering. He could tell her brain was busy working out the logistics, probably making plans to get even with her sister and stand him up at the same time.

"OK. I'll go out with you on one condition."

He tipped his head, surprised she'd agreed but wondering what stipulation she could possibly come up with to ruin the evening. "Name it."

"That I bring my nephew, Timmy. Since Sierra will be working for me, and she doesn't have a sitter for Friday nights, because Lance is in a bowling league, it's the least I can do."

Looking completely pleased with herself, she crossed her arms and tapped her clog, daring him to object.

Damn. A kid?

No way would he give China the satisfaction of thinking she'd gotten away with anything. He picked up Chad's chart and prepared to walk away.

"OK," he said. "If the kid comes, then we're having dinner at my place. He can play with my dogs. And for messing with my plans, I nominate you to cook."

He flapped the chart shut and returned to the ex-football star and his anxious parents, before China could utter a word in protest.

CHAPTER FOUR

CHINA grinned with pleasure. Rick lifted his eyebrows in surprise. Timmy's cowlick-ridden head bobbed up and down while he covered his mouth with a small hand and giggled. This was turning out to be some Friday night.

So far, the kid had beaten the big guy twice at checkers.

She hid her smile when Rick looked suspiciously at her.

"What kind of checker shark did you bring to my house, huh?" He made a playfully sinister glare at her six-year-old nephew.

Timmy stuck out his chest. "Play me again. Come on," he said with a raspy boyish voice. His face flushed red and his little mouth twisted with glee while he fought his laughter.

"Oh, yeah? Well, your Aunt China is going to have to barbeque the burgers while I'm whipping your, uh, bum."

"I'm going to whip yours," Timmy said, lining up his black checkers on the board.

OK, so she'd tried to pull a fast one on Rick by bringing her nephew to foil their date, and it had back-fired. Turnabout was fair play, even if it meant she'd have to cook.

China hated to miss the big event, though she had a pretty good hunch as to who would win yet again. Hunger pains and the thought of a home-cooked burger made her mouth water. She headed to the kitchen, stopping short to warn them.

"I don't want to hear any bickering or anyone accusing anyone else of cheating. Got that?" She made a stern "aunt" face, first for Timmy, then for Rick. When her gaze found Rick's, an odd sparkle in his eyes caught her off guard. Were those butterflies in her stomach? Nah, she was just hungry. She looked away and used the dogs for cover.

"Come on, girls," she called to Chloe and Jezebel, Rick's black Labrador retrievers. "Let's leave the boys to slug it out."

The dogs loped across the small living room and happily followed her through the kitchen door.

She thought she'd thrown Rick off track by insisting on bringing Timmy on their date, but so far he'd devoted one hundred per cent of his attention to her knobby-kneed, redheaded nephew. She had to admit it delighted her. It also touched her heart that he kept letting Timmy win at checkers. Who would have guessed he'd be so terrific with kids?

The big hunk from the ER had never let on there was a nurturing side to him before. Seeing him in a new light both perplexed and pleased China.

She gasped when she saw her goofy newsletter

picture hanging on his refrigerator, secured by a rainbow magnet. At least there wasn't a drawn-on mustache.

She washed her hands and noticed two sets of expectant eyes watching her every move. The dogs sat quietly while she formed the burger patties, placed them on a wax paper-lined plate and carried them outside. Rick had set everything up, and the coals were white hot and made a satisfying spitting sound when she put the meat onto the grill.

Another surprise grabbed her attention. Rick had potted plants, row after row of them, on his rustic wooden patio. The lawn was small but well manicured, and shrubs covered the height and length of the back fence. Unlike the flashy, in-your-face guy at work, his home was subdued, comfortable, and appealing.

Chloe whined, bringing China's attention back to the burgers. She looked over her shoulder. No one was looking. She threw an extra burger on the barbeque for the dogs to share, and winked. Chloe cocked her head, like she'd read her mind.

She flipped the meat just as Timmy made a triumphant outburst. "Woo-hoo! I beat you again."

The back door swung open, with Rick carrying Timmy over his shoulder like a sack of potatoes. She'd rarely seen her nephew laugh so hard. He kicked and squirmed, pretending to fight, but clearly loved every second of hanging upside down with drool pouring out of his mouth.

"Stop. Stop," he squealed.

Rick gently flopped her nephew onto the grass. "Get him, girls." Chloe and Jezebel romped over and began licking Timmy. The boy twisted into a ball and dissolved into laughter.

China smiled so widely her cheeks hurt. When was the last time that had happened?

Once Timmy and the dogs started playing Frisbee, Rick wandered over China's way. He wore broken in jeans and a snug T-shirt, and she couldn't help but notice how the clothes clung to his body. His cowboy boots were brown and well worn, unlike the fancy ones he'd had on the other night. He combed his hand through his rumpled brown hair, then took a deep whiff of the food and assumed a blissful expression. His broad grin made her knees go wobbly. She flipped the burgers again to distract herself.

"I'll wash up and grab the potato salad and buns," he said, with that same sparkle in his eyes he'd used on her earlier.

Welcoming his help, she pretended to ignore that look.

They ate outside on a wooden picnic table under a heat light and bug-zapper.

Zzzzt.

"Oh, another one bought it." A fascinated Timmy never grew tired of pointing it out, over and over and over.

China relaxed and enjoyed the scene. Everything felt natural here at Rick's house, which surprised her. At work, he always seemed to be "on." But here he was as natural as unpasteurized honey. She definitely preferred this Rick, though she had every plan to keep him at a safe distance.

Rick cleared the table and, without thinking twice,

China jumped up to help. Timmy went back to bug-watching and Frisbee-throwing with the dogs.

No sooner had they reached the sink than the doorbell rang. Rick wiped his hands on his thighs and strode to the front door.

"Hey, D'Wayne. Come in."

He escorted a baggy-clothed, backward-ballcap-wearing teenager with dreadlocks into the kitchen, and made introductions all around.

"You hungry? I'll grill a burger for you." Rick didn't give the kid a chance to answer. He grabbed the meat from the refrigerator and had a patty made in a beat. "Get yourself a soda while I put this on." He pushed through the door to the grill.

By the easy way he found his drink, D'Wayne was no stranger to Rick's kitchen. Timmy had come back inside and followed the teenager's every move in awe. He cast a half-smile at her nephew. "What up, little dude?"

Timmy turned suddenly shy, but followed him out back.

Though reserved around China, D'Wayne opened up with Rick outside. Through the back door, she listened to their basketball conversation about the Lakers' latest losing streak, while she washed the dishes.

When she'd finished, she brought two cans of soda outside—a refill for D'Wayne and one for Rick.

Rick sat across from the teen, giving him his full attention. "So how's school going?"

D'Wayne got quiet. "Well, I went every day this week."

Rick nodded with approval, looking impressed. "Do any homework?"

D'Wayne made a sheepish look. "Some."

"Well, there you go. Keep it up."

D'Wayne fought a smile, and drank some more soda.

"Where are you heading tonight?" Rick asked.

"Nowhere. Just kickin' back." He looked over his shoulder, checking out where China was.

She got the distinct impression that D'Wayne had something on his mind, and wasn't about to open up with an audience.

"Would it be OK if Timmy and I walked the dogs?" she asked.

"I think they'd like that," Rick said, with an appreciative glance.

Timmy jumped up from watching the bug-zapper, excited. "I get to walk Jezebel, OK, Aunt China?"

She helped him put the leashes on both dogs, and they exited with animals in tow through the back-yard gate.

A half-hour later Timmy was dragging his feet, but the dogs were still raring to go. China checked her watch. After nine. Definitely past his bedtime. They strolled up the path to Rick's door just as D'Wayne and Rick were involved in a complicated handshake that ended with knocking knuckles.

"Wow," Timmy said, fascinated.

"I'm proud of you D'Wayne," Rick said.

"Yeah." D'Wayne almost smiled. He nodded to Timmy and China when he passed them. "Think I'll go home and watch some tube."

"I'll see you Sunday morning, OK? We'll work on that English paper."

"Yeah."

"You sure you don't need a lift to the bus stop?"

"Nah." He wandered down the street looking like he had nothing in particular to do.

His full attention back to China, Rick smiled as they went inside. "Good walk?"

She nodded. "So tell me how a guy like you knows a kid like D'Wayne."

"I'm in a big brother program. He got assigned to me. D'Wayne's come a long way in the last year."

What else would Rick pull out of his bag of tricks?

"He just told me he was invited to a party where he knew there'd be drugs and alcohol, and he decided to come visit me instead."

"That's fantastic," she said.

They looked at each other for several seconds. His eyes glided over her mouth and hair. She glanced away before she could get that butterfly feeling again. They'd managed to spend several hours together without any effort, aside from intense, lingering glances, yet had kept their distance. She'd made sure of that, and she wasn't anywhere near ready to scale the divide.

On the couch, Timmy yawned and rubbed his eyes. Relieved by the distraction, and on the verge of breaking the inevitable news, she cleared her throat. "It's time to take Timmy home and put him to bed."

As if on cue, there was a light tap on the front door. China assumed D'Wayne had returned for that lift to the bus stop, and was surprised when Rick opened the door to her sister.

"Hi, Mommy," Timmy ran across the room and hugged her leg.

"Hey, squirt." She bent to give him a tight hug.

"What are you doing here?" China asked, incredulous.

"They were overstaffed tonight, so I volunteered to leave early."

China crossed her arms. "Oh, really. Good thing you happened to know Rick's address." She glanced at Rick, who wore a poker face. "I can't believe I fell for this set-up."

Rick raised his hands. "I swear I had nothing to do with it. But I must compliment Sierra on her thoroughness." He grinned, and ruffled Timmy's hair. "Well, it was great meeting you kid."

Sierra smirked apologetically at China.

She shook her head. Oh, the vicious webs Sierra could weave when it came to fixing her kid sister up with a date.

Timmy smiled at Rick, showing off a missing front tooth. "I liked kicking your bum."

"Yeah? Well, next time I'm going to kick your butt."

Sierra lifted a brow, took Timmy by the hand and said goodnight, leaving China feeling nervous for the first time in the entire evening.

"May I get you a drink?" Rick asked, switching on music and heading for the kitchen.

She half expected him to lower the lights, too.

Angry, but not quite feeling trapped, China made a quick decision. "I'd like some herbal tea, if you don't mind."

Trying hard to ignore the sweet and sexy jazz saxophone music he'd put on, she sat on the couch and crossed her denim-clad legs.

His living room reflected a man's taste—dark leather furniture, smoked glass over a varnished tree-stump coffee-table, with recessed lighting casting a warm glow over the stark white walls, and several framed classic-car posters.

A picture of an older woman was placed in a key spot on the nearest bookcase. His mother? She had kind eyes, a sweet smile, and loads of deep brown hair. Rick had inherited all of it.

She glanced around the room, but couldn't find a picture of his father anywhere.

Rick clanked and banged around the kitchen, opening drawers and cupboards, until a whistle signaled the water had boiled for her tea.

A moment later Rick pushed through the kitchen door with a tray complete with two mugs and steeping teabags, cookies, and what looked like two dog biscuits. She'd always sworn you could tell a lot about a man by the way he treated animals. From the looks of Chloe and Jezebel, Rick was a damn nice guy, a fact she wasn't any where near ready to deal with.

Looking smug, he placed everything on the coffee-table and sat next to her. Only then did she realize how good he smelled, like spicy soap and chamomile tea.

"There's only one thing wrong with tonight," he said as he relaxed into the comfortable couch next to her.

"Really?"

He glanced at her sports shoes.

"You're not wearing those sexy, slinky shoes you had on the other night." He popped a cookie into his mouth and crunched. "It hurts to know that underneath those sensible shoes are two perfectly beautiful feet with red polish on adorable toes, yet you selfishly keep them to yourself." He shook his head. "Cruel."

How could he have seen her feet and high-heeled sandals on Saturday night? She'd gone out of her way to avoid him the rest of the night at the charity event.

"Cookie?" he offered.

Chocolate—who could resist? She accepted and nibbled.

Chloe and Jezebel came sniffing around and he made them sit and shake his hand with their paws before he gave them their biscuits. She caught herself smiling and put a quick end to it.

"I hope you realize that this evening doesn't qualify for the date I purchased."

She lifted a brow in mid-bite.

"I bought a special date. You have to get dressed up. Wear those sexy shoes. And we'll go to a fancy dinner by the ocean."

Fighting a sudden urge to run for the hills, she sipped some tea. "Listen, Rick." She swallowed the rest of her cookie. "You don't have to take me out and drop a lot of your hard-earned money. I'm just grateful you contributed what you did for a great cause."

"Sorry, no can do," he said, with determination in his dark brown eyes. "I bought a date, and I expect a date. Besides, I want to get to know the real China Seabury. The one you keep locked away behind your crusader façade."

His gaze sent a shiver to her core.

She tensed.

"I bet you didn't think I knew 'façade', did you?"

She smirked, wondering how he knew exactly what she'd been thinking.

"I'm just talking dinner," he said. "Don't worry."

"Why do you want to do this?" He was totally out of her league. Did he have some twisted bet with someone or, worse yet, a vendetta to repay? What had she ever done to him, other than ignore him?

"In case you haven't noticed, China, you're an interesting woman." His dark, knowing gaze startled her. "I think you work too hard, fundraise too much, crusade non-stop, and, hell, you deserve a break. You're moody and tough to get along with, but I think there's something you're hiding, and I'm curious to find out what it is."

China tensed. She'd spent years skillfully concealing her guilt and shame. Was she that transparent?

"And, to be honest, I think we've got a lot in common."

She sputtered in mid-sip of tea. "Us?"

A taunting smile spread across his face. "Yes, us."

"I don't mean to be rude, but I think you're nuts. We couldn't be more different if we tried."

Her negative attitude didn't faze him. He just grinned, annoyingly.

"I like a challenge," he said.

He'd gotten under her skin enough for a lifetime, and now was the time to make her break. She stood up. "Thank you for dinner and the tea. I almost enjoyed myself."

There was no need to be rude, but she was scared.

Why had she started to retreat? A strange disappointment niggled in the back of her mind. The thought of snuggling on Rick's couch and watching a DVD seemed oddly appealing. What the hell was she thinking? Snuggling led to closeness, and closeness led

to heartbreak. She'd traveled down that road already.
Not to mention the constant knowledge of how little she
deserved that factored into her every thought, in every
moment, of every day. Never again would she be open
to any kind of personal relationship, especially with
someone like Rick.

There seemed to be two Ricks—the brazen charmer
at work, and the unplugged home version, definitely the
more appealing of the two. What was a girl to believe?
Did he really want to get to know her? Or just have her
and run?

China searched for her purse, totally bewildered.

Rick strolled to the front door and pushed it open.
He stared at her with a thoughtful gaze, as if calling her
bluff. His warm brown eyes almost melted her resolve
to dislike him.

She followed his lead, and walked toward the door,
wishing things could be different yet utterly torn
between her natural instinct to protect herself and good
judgement. Was she making a mistake by leaving?

She sensed his desire when she reached him. Chills
started at the crown of her head and fell like a water-
fall down her spine to her toes. Using all of her resolve
to ignore the lure, she stepped passed him. Just when
she thought she'd made it home free, he reached for her
arm and turned her around.

"You're a terrible actress."

Looking into his eyes, she saw intensity and
longing that matched her own. It frightened her.
"What do you mean?"

"You don't want to leave any more than I want
you to."

In that instant she knew he intended to kiss her and, surprisingly, she wanted to kiss him back. Her pulse tripled its beat, and her breathing went haywire.

He grasped her arms and tugged her close. Now the thought of resisting didn't cross her mind. An odd excitement sent a shiver to her bones as his mouth covered hers in a warm, inviting kiss.

Her lips softened and welcomed his in a fashion she hadn't felt for many years. Her hands crept up his shoulders and around his neck, absorbing the wondrous sensation of heat and strength. His fingers splayed across her back and shoulders, keeping her snug in his embrace. She relished the sensation, and took a deep, relaxing breath before teasing and inviting his tongue into her mouth. The soft, velvety feel and herbal tea taste took her breath away.

Was it wise to kiss a man who wanted to know her secrets? What was she doing? Oh, hell, who cared? This was too good.

She gave in, went woozy, and the earth stirred beneath her feet. Amazed, she shook while braced in the deep, luscious kiss. The floor shifted under her.

Wow.

It wasn't her imagination.

They parted lips and discovered, much to their surprise, a genuine earthquake. They locked into a surprised stare, testing reality in each other's eyes. The doorway shook and rattled for a few seconds, then settled down.

Fear enveloped her, as her pulse bounded through her chest.

"That was one hell of a kiss." He tried to sound casual, but fell short. "We made the earth move."

She gave a nervous laugh. Edgy, she held onto Rick. He embraced her protectively, and comforted her with a peck on the top of her head.

"Don't worry. It's just a small one."

No sooner had he said it than a rumbling started in the distance and grew until it rolled through the house, jiggling and shaking everything inside. The gyrating earth turned quickly to jackhammer vibrations, banging fiercely on the foundations of his house.

China felt as if a giant was trying to shake her out of a box. And a loud eerie sound, something she'd never heard before, assaulted her ears, as though a roaring locomotive drove through Rick's yard.

Lights flashed. Glass broke and shattered. Furniture fell into the center of his living room.

Crashing.

Banging.

Shaking.

They were thrown off his front porch to the ground.

Fear grabbed hold, disorienting her, making her stomach go queasy. She screamed.

He covered her body with his own to protect her from flying debris. They scrambled to their knees, ran and huddled together in his front yard, watching out for falling branches. Her heart quivered and her palms went damp with alarm.

The shaking and trembling continued for what seemed like an eternity. And then, as quickly as it had begun, it stopped.

Haunting stillness.

An odd silence replaced the chaos.

China looked at Rick, who scanned the yard and

house. He pulled her to her feet and gave her a reassuring look. Cautiously, she returned a half-hearted smile, though her pulse still raced.

Neighbors ran out of their houses and into the streets, talking fast and calling to friends.

"That felt like a 6 or more," one neighbor announced.

China agreed. The tumbler had seemed to last close to a minute. She knew the longer an earthquake went on the higher the Richter scale reading.

Jezebel and Chloe rushed out of the house to find Rick. They barked, terror in their eyes. He held them and tried to settle them down while checking if they had any injuries. Holding onto their collars, he whistled through his teeth and called to his next-door neighbor.

"Hey, Nick. You okay?"

"Yeah," Nick said. "Everything OK with you?"

"We're OK. Hey, man. I need to ask you a favor."

"Shoot."

"Once I've turned off my gas and water, I'm going to have to report to the hospital. Can you keep the dogs for me?"

"Sure, you know I will." Nick strode over, bent down and petted both of the panting dogs. They seemed to respond to him, as though they knew him well.

China could read the hesitation in Rick's eyes about leaving his pets so soon after something as stressful as an earthquake, but she also knew, as well as he did, that it was necessary.

She thought about Timmy, Sierra, Lance, and her mother. Were they OK? What damage had their houses sustained? Was anyone hurt?

A million thoughts rushed through her head, not the least of which was a mystified realization that Rick Morell wasn't at all what he appeared to be. But there was no time now to ponder what that meant.

Any dedicated medical professional worth their salt reported to work after a natural disaster. With power outages and broken glass, the number-one injury would be cuts and lacerations, not to mention broken bones from people stumbling through the dark, or having furniture fall on them, and much worse injuries. She shivered at the thought. The ER would be crawling with patients. And the hospital would be on Code Orange disaster alert.

Counting her blessings for avoiding a close call with a deviously attractive man, she pretended not to be disappointed. She brushed herself off, and prepared for the long night ahead.

"After I shut things up here, we'll go by your house and turn your gas and water off, OK?"

She nodded, following him, numbly wondering what damage she'd find at her apartment, glad to have Rick at her side.

"Then we'll report for duty."

She agreed wholeheartedly with him.

He turned, and with a tug on her hand he pulled her forward to look squarely into her eyes.

"And after everything is over, and things have settled down, we'll get back to you and me."

She stopped dead in her tracks and thought she felt the earth move again.

CHAPTER FIVE

CHINA and Rick pushed through a crowd of stunned and animated people gathered in front of Mercy Hospital. Boisterous with anxiety, the throng pressed onward, impatiently waiting for casualty triage. They made their way up to the entrance where a temporary command post had been erected in the hospital lobby.

Spotting the night-shift nursing supervisor, who manned one of the tables, China waved and navigated through more people, edging closer to the front. The nurse was busily assessing a misshapen forearm.

"Looks like a fractured radius. You need to go to Radiology, the orange station." She pointed in the direction.

China and Rick inched closer to the table.

"Excuse me," China said to the annoyed man blocking her path. "I work here."

"We're reporting for duty," Rick added, using a warm hand on the small of her back as he protectively guided her around the unmoving male.

The nurse looked frazzled. "Hi. I'm so glad you're

OK. I got picked for first-line triage," she said quickly, with wide, adrenaline-washed eyes.

China could barely hear her over the noisy crowd.

"Are you OK?" China had never felt particularly close to the woman, but under the circumstances wanted to reach out and hug her.

The nurse nodded as they briefly touched hands. Someone pushed against China, and Rick stepped between her and the rest of the crowd.

He raised his voice. "Everyone, please, be patient. We'll evaluate your injuries and send you to the proper areas for treatment as quickly as possible."

Several other hospital managers and administrators lined the long table, walkie-talkies in hand.

"Please, folks," one said. "Stay calm and be patient. We're doing the best we can. You will all be seen tonight." His voice was assuring and authoritative. "Be patient."

"Can you believe what a mess things are?" China grasped the nurse's hands and clung tightly. The nurse blinked back a trace of tears. "It was horrible. I thought the hospital was going to collapse."

China remembered the shocking sight of her apartment. Nothing had been left standing. Everything she owned seemed to have been thrown into a pile in the middle of the living-room floor. Her kitchen was a heap of broken dishes and rapidly defrosting food. She avoided the thought of eventually going home and dealing with it. Remembering feeling like the earth would swallow her up at Rick's house, she could imagine what the hospital must have been like during the earthquake.

She glanced around the lobby, normally clean and

functional. Everything was in disarray. Clean-up crews worked efficiently sweeping up debris. Several engineers scuttled around, large flashlights in hand, calling out orders to each other, and taping a big orange "X" across the elevators.

"I guess the earthquake retrofitting we did sure paid off," China said. "Things are messed up, but at least the hospital is still standing and functional."

"Yeah," Rick said. "It could have been a lot worse. Looks like things are getting under control."

"As long as the back-up generator holds up." The nurse forced a smile. "Thanks for coming in, guys."

China opened her mouth to respond when the hospital administrator appeared.

"Listen, China, we can use you in the ambulatory station." She scanned her clipboard. "That's the green station in the urgent care area." She glanced up. "It's for minor lacerations, minimal treatments. Any impaired function goes to the ER. If the UCC overflows, we'll use the conference room down the hall."

Her eyes fell on Rick. "Oh, great. We can use you in the goldenrod station. Immediate stabilization in the ER." The walkie-talkie she held squawked.

China glanced at Rick, preparing to say goodbye. He offered a reassuring smile and rubbed her shoulder. The gesture, though small, gave her confidence that she could handle whatever lay ahead.

"Oh, hey," the administrator broke in. "First, can you two help out with patient movement?" The short, stout woman didn't waste any time changing assignments. "The fifth floor has suffered extreme damage and we need to evacuate the remaining ventilator patients."

The confidence that she could handle whatever was thrown at her wobbled a little.

Rick grabbed her wrist with a strong hand. "We're on it."

Just before they left, a very pregnant lady appeared at the head of the line. "She's in labor," the man beside her said in a loud and strained voice.

"Get a wheelchair," the commanding administrator said to one of the assistants. "Take her to the purple station, obstetrics, first floor."

"Down this way," Rick said. "Follow us."

China and Rick crossed the foyer, dodging some overturned vases and potted plants. The dim back-up lighting forced them to move cautiously. China followed Rick's sure-footed path past the elevators to the stairs.

"It's right down this hall," he said, smiling encouragingly at the husband and pregnant wife.

A temporary purple arrow pointed the way to the assigned obstetrics triage area.

When Rick opened the door to the stairwell, China focused on his boots and denim clad legs and followed suit. Taking the steps two at a time, she managed to keep up with him until the third floor. She yanked her hand free, bursting for breath.

"Hold on," she gasped. "I won't be able to help if I die first." Her thighs were already tightening up, reacting to Rick's athletic lead up the stairs. She placed her hands on her hips and worked to steady her breathing. The air was stuffy and the stairwell hot.

He stopped abruptly. "I'm sorry, I guess I got too focused. It's like a war zone here. I slipped into military mode."

Too many months of planning meetings after work, instead of time at the gym, had left her out of shape. But eager to help, she inhaled the stale air and sprinted up the next flight of stairs, leaving Rick in her wake.

They reached the fifth floor to find it eerie and darker than the lobby. A solitary stressed-out nurse with a flashlight greeted them. "We're over here."

Two orderlies rolled portable oxygen tanks across the deserted nurses' station.

Rick burst on the scene like a tornado. "How many patients are left? Where are they?"

"Two," the nurse replied. "Rooms 5003 and 5007, the private rooms."

"Who is the sickest?"

"5007."

Rick ran to the entrance. China padded quickly behind. The room housed a comatose young female patient who must have weighed close to three hundred pounds.

"We'll move 5003 first."

Rick ran to the bedside of the first patient, a frail old man, just as an aftershock rocked the floor.

China tensed and stood perfectly still. Fighting a surge of terror, she scanned the hospital ward, searching for a safe place to take shelter, deciding to dive under the nurses' station desk. She didn't breathe until a few seconds later when the shaking stopped. She ventured back to the room in time to hear Rick console the patient.

"We're going to move you down to the ER holding area. You'll be safe there." He'd padded the man's head with a pillow to protect him from any fallout during the shaker.

She stepped up to the bedside and saw a gaunt face and dark eyes dart anxiously from her to Rick and back. She stroked his bony hand.

"We'll take good care of you. We promise." She smiled, first at the patient and then at Rick.

For a millisecond their eyes met, and he gave an appreciative smile, one you'd expect from an old friend, an old, sexy friend, causing a quick burst of adrenaline in her chest. She looked away rather than deal with her awakening feelings.

"Get the adult ambubag from the crash cart," Rick said, over his shoulder. The first orderly sprinted across the room.

"We'll use a two-man carry to transport this patient. China? You'll man the ambubag once we've removed Mr...." he looked at the patient's wristband and squinted in the dim emergency back-up lights "...Mr. Aziz, from the ventilator." Rick eyed the first young orderly who'd just returned with the portable oxygen. "You and I will carry him. I'll take the head, you take the feet. China, you'll stay by me and assist with his respirations. OK?"

The orderly nodded, already moving into position. China did the same.

Mr. Aziz flashed a look of terror. Rick bent close to his face and looked him squarely in the eyes. "Sir, this lovely nurse..." he pointed across the bed to China, and the patient moved his eyes slowly her way "...is going to replace the ventilator. She'll make sure you get plenty of oxygen."

The other orderly jogged back with the ambubag, handing it to China. She held it so Mr. Aziz could examine it. "See? I'll use this respirator to breathe for you. You'll be fine."

Once she saw the anxiety ease from his tense face, she connected the tubing to the portable oxygen tank and cranked it up to 15 liters. After removing the ventilator tubing, she placed the ambubag firmly over the patient's tracheostomy, and nodded for Rick to shut down the ventilator.

He followed her command before the machine had a chance to make one beep of warning. The room suddenly went quiet after the ventilator took its last mechanized breath.

On cue, China used both hands to compress the large bellows over the patient's windpipe.

One and two and three and let go. One and two and three and four and five. Compress, again, for three. Relax for five.

The other orderly placed the oxygen canister next to the patient on the sheet for easier transport.

Rick removed the IV from the bedside infusion machine. He adjusted the flow to a keep-open rate, and placed it on the patient's trunk, then put the urine catheter bag between the patient's legs. Turning off the bedside monitor, he removed the leads from the man's malnourished chest.

Using the draw sheet, Rick anchored the oxygen tank tightly to the patient's trunk by knotting the ends around his torso.

"Are you all set?" he asked Mr. Aziz, before he made the final move.

When the elderly man nodded his OK, Rick tucked his forearms under the patient's armpits and used his chest to support the head and shoulders. The orderly slid Mr. Aziz's feet to the edge of the mattress. Rick pointed out something to the orderly, and he replaced a thin hospital slipper on one of the patient's sock-covered feet in final preparation for the lift.

On the count of three, the patient was in the air and being moved out of the room.

China focused on the job at hand and followed closely beside the two-man team. Rick and the orderly, doing the hardest part, carried the snugly wrapped patient toward the stairway.

She continued her ministrations with the equipment, making sure the patient was properly oxygenated. The frail, elderly man looked at her with dilated pupils and tension in his eyes. She tried to give him a reassuring smile, but her lips quivered.

"We've got you. Don't worry," came Rick's confident voice.

She felt his solid strength each time she compressed the bellows of the ambubag. Like a rock, he moved steadily across the hospital ward, giving her silent reassurance, for which both she and Mr. Aziz, judging by the eased look in his eyes, were grateful.

When they arrived at the stairway, it got crowded. The other nurse and orderly opened the door, having planned to stay behind with the remaining patient. The orderly helping them took the feet first, holding each one through the loop of his muscular arm in a partial piggyback hold. China had to squeeze herself between the wall and Rick to keep in touch with the mask and her patient in the narrow stairwell. She kept at a three-quarter forward facing position to help maneuver down the stairs safely, afraid her weakened legs might give out. After five surgical procedures and two years of rehab, the last thing she needed was to miss a step and fall down a flight of stairs.

Slowly but surely they made it down each of the five flights of stairs to the ground floor, and eventually to the ER.

To their amazement, a stopgap station had been prepared for the patient, complete with a narrow gurney and a portable ventilator.

A respiratory therapist took over for China, allowing her to stretch her back and shake out her aching hands and legs. She was grateful she hadn't worn the shoes Rick had been so disappointed about earlier. Nothing like sports shoes for hard work.

A firm hand pressed against her waist. "Why don't you head over to your station?" Rick said, causing a rush of tingles to shoot up her spine. With concern in his eyes, he searched her face. "I'm bringing Chuck here to help with that last transport."

She glanced at the physically fit, middle-aged male ER nurse, and made a snap decision. "OK."

Rick smiled, and for the briefest moment China thought he might lean in and kiss her again before he left. That aggravating sparkle in his eyes made it both hard and easy to say goodbye. She squirmed under his scrutiny and said, "You'd better get going."

"I'll see you later," he said, with more confidence than she could take.

She tossed her head and rolled her eyes, with an "as if" attitude. It only made him grin more.

Amidst controlled chaos, she watched the nurse and

the orderly, but especially Rick, exit the room. His broad shoulders and narrow hips were a sight to behold. A warm blush tickled up her cheeks. What was he doing to her good sense?

Changing directions and shaking her head, she wondered how in the world the lift team would manage to get the last patient—obese and comatose—down five flights of stairs and into the ER without anyone getting a back injury.

And she worried about Rick.

At five a.m. China needed a break. She'd worked non-stop in the urgent care section, cleaning cuts, dressing larger wounds, even stitching up a patient or two.

Her legs and hips ached, and she needed water and fuel for energy. She wandered to the bank of fast-food machines on the outskirts of the nurses' lounge and dropped a few quarters in.

"I've heard that if you eat enough of that junk food, it can kill you."

Thrilled to hear Rick's voice again, she turned with a smile. He returned the favor with a dashing grin, and handed her a bottle of water.

"Thanks."

"Things have settled down in the ER and the night shift is taking over now, so why don't we take a break?" He reached for her hand and laced his fingers through hers, leading her to the cafeteria.

The code orange team had done an impeccable job of setting things up. Cots with folded blankets were placed around the periphery of the large room, allowing exhausted hospital workers to rest for brief periods of time. Several employees were doing so now. The lights were dim, and China walked quietly so as not to disturb them.

Rick whisked by one of the vacant cots and snatched up a blanket with his free hand. Both drawn to and leery of his commanding lead, she followed him to the corner of the cafeteria where a long booth lined the wall.

"Sit," he said, dropping her hand.

She immediately missed the heat of his grasp. Too tired to protest, she sat like she'd been told, on the stain-resistant, burnt-orange cafeteria bench.

A few minutes later he came back with two cups of hot coffee and a bag of mixed nuts. China had unwrapped her granola bar, broken it in two and offered half to Rick. He popped the oats and honey morsel into his mouth in one bite and chomped away.

She sipped her coffee, amazed that somewhere along the way he'd noticed she took cream and no sugar.

"How'd you know?" She lifted her styrofoam cup.

"ER lounge. I only look like I'm oblivious to the world. Nothing much gets by me." He smiled. "It's my military training."

"Gosh," was all she could think of to say. She took a sip then nibbled on a cashew. "So tell me, how'd you guys get that comatose patient down to the ER?"

He laughed and took a swig of his steaming coffee. "You won't believe what happened." He popped a few nuts into his mouth and chewed vigorously. "We used a gurney, and it took four of us, plus the nurse who was bagging the patient, to get her to the stairwell. We'd strapped her on the gurney to keep her from sliding, since we'd decided to glide her down the stairs."

His dazzling brown eyes captured her full attention. Amazed at her new burst of energy from just sitting next to Rick, China prompted him with a go-on grin.

"You know what I like about you?" he said.

Her smile tightened at the thought of things getting personal. He didn't wait for her answer his rhetorical question.

"When you smile, you put your tongue behind your teeth. That's really cute."

Her face blazed with embarrassment, and she shut her mouth.

"Now I've ruined it." He cleared his throat, gave a scowl of disappointment and got back on target. "Anyway, we'd managed to get the patient to the third floor when we heard the engineers announce over the PA system that the elevators had been inspected and were good to go again." He grinned. "You mean you didn't hear us cheer in the stairwell? We almost woke up the comatose lady."

She laughed, and shook her head, enjoying every second of watching Rick. His expressive dark eyes, wavy brown hair, strong jaw and, oh, that cleft in his chin were almost more than she could bear.

He caught her appreciation, revelled in the exchange and finally continued. "Yeah. So we exited the nearest landing and hitched a ride on the elevator the rest of the way down." He covered her hand and played with her fingers. "She's fine," he said reassuringly. "She'll be fine."

One look and China realized that Rick really did give a damn about his patients. He'd proved that over and over during the long night. Somehow she knew that he would have done whatever it took to get that woman where she needed to be. Unthinking, she squeezed his hand. He rubbed his thumb across her knuckles.

Chills shot up her arm and fanned across her chest.

"You look really tired," he said, concern in his eyes. "I don't have to tell you how hard it's been."

His hand brushed her cheek and caught a wisp of hair between his thumb and forefinger. He curled it around his finger and studied it intently for a second before smiling at her, as if he wanted to give her a hug.

She got lost in his deep, dark eyes, and before she could prepare herself he blindsided her with a kiss, again.

He pulled her close and pressed his lips to hers for one quick beat. Immediately caught up in the moment, she was surprised when he moved back and looked into her eyes, as if making sure she was OK with his kiss.

Oh, yeah. She was more than OK with kissing him. She'd stopped several times during the course of the night, remembering how heavenly it had felt when they'd kissed at his house. Each time chills had shot up her spine with the memory. When had that happened, ever?

She chased his lips with her own and kissed him back. He moaned quietly, and when it was apparent that she didn't mind, he opened his mouth and covered hers. His tongue darted into her eager mouth, and her hands flew up to his neck. She tangled her fingers through his thick hair. His breath was hot across her face. He teased and withdrew, only to dive in again for more and deeper kisses.

She groaned, and briefly thought about the fact that they were in the hospital cafeteria, but cast the thought right out of her head, savoring his touch and deciding that after the earthquake it could be considered extenuating circumstances. If anyone intended to practice good sense, it would have to be him, definitely not her. Not now.

She'd just captured his lower lip between hers when she felt him pull back. His hooded, intent eyes flashed a warning. One more step, and there would be no turning back.

Coming to her senses, as though climbing through a fog, China forced the voice of reason into her mind.

Not here. Not now.

And to emphasize the point, Mother Nature threw her two cents in. A mild aftershock vibrated the table and booth. She bit her lower lip, sighed and looked longingly into his eyes.

He cleared his throat and pressed his forehead to hers.

"Damn," he said. "What am I going to do with you?"

Her own inner earthquake helped her sober up. She moved away and sipped her coffee, feeling suddenly prim. "I could ask the same question."

"Well, here's a novel idea. Why don't we take a nap? You look exhausted, honey."

She pinched his cheek. "What'd I tell you about calling me that?"

He raised his hands in surrender and grinned. "I can't help it, the name suits you."

She gave him an incredulous stare. "Never in my life have I ever done anything warranting that name."

"Not yet, anyway." He gave an over-confident, knowing grin and took another sip of coffee.

Wanting to take offense, China tried her best to feel insulted. Instead, deep tingling coursed through her core. How was she supposed to be able to sleep now?

Rick angled himself into the corner of the cafeteria booth. He lifted one leg onto the bench and motioned for China to snuggle in with him.

"Come on. I won't bite." Looking worn out, with deep-set, tired eyes, he grinned. "I might nibble a little on your earlobe, but I promise I won't bite."

Against her better judgement, China turned and shifted and edged her way between the V of his legs. And after a great deal of adjustment she allowed herself to rest against the firm expanse of his chest, using his shoulder as her pillow.

His strong arms encircled her and held her tight. She nuzzled her head between his chin and shoulder and, completely exhausted, dared to relax for the first time that night.

He covered both of them with the blanket, and an odd feeling crept up her spine. She felt completely and utterly safe. Soaking in his warmth and solid chest, along with every fiber of his masculinity, she sighed, amazed by the secure feeling.

An unwelcome longing for a normal life, the life she'd expected to have with her fiancé just before he'd dumped her three years ago, made her tense up. It had been a fool's dream anyway, one she'd never achieve.

Taking the cue from her vulnerability, old guilt whispered, You don't deserve this. Why should you be happy? She gritted her teeth and stayed completely still, waiting for the familiar feelings of dread to pass.

Within seconds Rick had gone silent and still. His

deep, even breathing lulled her to rest. Focusing on the here and now, and pushing old torment aside, she let her tension go, as if launching a boat. Soon she managed to follow him across the inviting, lazy river of rest toward sleep.

A mild aftershock and a shadow blocking the sun from the cafeteria window woke Rick. Memories of an earthquake came into focus before his eyes could. The disapproving stare from his father made him sit bolt upright, alerting China.

With stubborn resolve he willed himself to move slowly, rubbing his hand through his disheveled hair. He was damned if he'd give his father any satisfaction about taking him by surprise.

China stirred from her position snuggling close to his chest.

He smoothed her hair and looked lazily at his father. He stretched, feigning nonchalance, while defiance set in.

"Why, good morning, Father. What brings you to the eating place of common employees?"

"All things considered, I believe your break is up," Dr. Morell replied.

CHAPTER SIX

THE next few days were a blur. China worked double shifts over the weekend, and spent the rest of her time sorting through and cleaning up her non-earthquake-proofed apartment. She and Rick only glimpsed each other while going in or out of ER cubicles at work.

Dr. Morell had made sure both she and Rick knew how displeased he was with finding them asleep together in the hospital cafeteria the morning after the earthquake. No amount of explaining had appeased him. Rick had finally stood up, looked him square in the eye and had told him he didn't give a damn what he thought, and to butt out of his personal life.

The head of Internal Medicine had given a steel-cold stare, turned on his heel, and left, leaving China praying she wouldn't run into him at work in the near future or, for that matter, ever again.

By Wednesday, things began to settle down in the ER, except for the hospital engineers' constant presence. They'd finally packed up their gray carts and bright orange ladders and cleared out for the evening when a mild aftershock reminded everyone that, regardless of how prepared they may be, Mother Nature was still in charge.

"Three point five," one doctor called out in the casual manner they'd all grown accustomed to since the earthquake had hit.

"That had to be a five," a nurse answered with a tense smile. "I don't feel them unless they're five or more."

"Four point seven," another nurse joined in, sounding like a judge at the Olympics.

China and Rick happened to meet up at the nurses' station. She needed an intake and output sheet, and he was answering a phone call. She checked her tight French twist with a fluttering hand and crossed her arms to cover the nervous jitters he'd evoked. She'd pretend the earthquake had made her anxious, not him.

He hung up the phone, smiled broadly and sauntered up beside her. "How've you been?" He nudged her with his shoulder.

Her cheeks got hot. "Fine. I finally have my apartment back in living order. How about you?"

"Almost there."

"Chloe? Jezebel?"

"Nervous, but fine. So, now that you've cleaned up your apartment, maybe you'll invite me over?"

Sierra popped her head outside one of the cubicles across the room. "China?"

China straightened, wishing she had more time to shoot the breeze with Rick. Offering an apologetic smile, she said, "Gotta go."

Rick nodded, and she was positive he watched her walk away, forcing her to pretend that her weak leg wasn't bothering her.

When she entered the patient's room, Sierra's eyes were wide with bewilderment.

"What's up?" China asked.

Sierra lifted her hands and shrugged her shoulders. "He's gone."

"Who's gone?"

"My patient. I brought him in here to change into a hospital gown, pulled the curtain and left to get his chart." Sierra shook her head in disbelief. "No one left this room. I'm sure of it."

China stuck her head outside the door. "Anyone see a patient leave?"

Several heads, including Rick's, lifted from various locations in the large central station, blank looks all around. No one had noticed anything.

She returned to the room to find Sierra staring dumbfounded at the ceiling. The engineers hadn't replaced the heater vent in the ceiling. An approximate fifteen by fifteen inch square opening gaped at them. She followed her gaze back to the gurney lined up beneath it. Two waffled footprints were in evidence.

China whistled through her teeth. "You gotta be kidding me."

"The guy was very nervous," Sierra said. "He said he'd cut his arm during the earthquake over the weekend. I assessed him briefly and it looked like he'd developed cellulitis. I told him to change his clothes to a hospital gown so a doctor could examine him." She kept shaking her head with a baffled look. "You don't suppose…" She glanced upward.

China crawled onto the gurney and stood on tiptoe, but still couldn't reach the vent portal. "How tall was he?"

"He was a wiry guy, about five-ten."

"Do you honestly think he could have made it inside?"

"How the heck should I know?" Sierra said, in a strained whisper. "Why would he do that? This is too weird."

"What's his name?"

"Peter."

China cupped her hands around her mouth. "Peter?" She called toward the ceiling. No answer. She hopped down from the gurney. "I'm getting Rick."

On her way out she grabbed the patient chart and waved Rick over, trying not to call attention to the situation.

He wandered toward her with his usual ER love-to-be-needed smile securely in place. "At your service, ladies."

"We have a situation here," China said with a strained whisper, and tossed her head toward cubicle number three.

He grinned. "A situation?"

"Sierra's patient has gone missing, and we think he crawled into the ceiling air vent."

He sputtered a laugh, and she shushed him.

"I don't want to alarm anyone until we know for sure," she whispered. "Maybe I should call Security?"

"Let me have a look." He took the chart from her hand and glanced at the name. A lightning flash of recognition crossed his face, and he glanced up with a quizzical look. "Peter Wexler? This is the guy that thought Mr. Boots was stalking him. He's a paranoid schizophrenic. Damn."

He put the chart in the door holder and rushed inside the room.

China followed quickly behind. "Maybe the aftershock scared him?"

"Who knows? It could be anything." Rick hopped onto the gurney, reached up and tested the vent for stability. Agile as an athlete, he pulled himself into a chinup until his head disappeared. "Peter?" He hung from the ceiling for a few moments before he lowered himself. "I think I saw movement. I'm going in."

Sierra gasped.

China's heart sank to her stomach. Before she could protest, Rick was halfway inside the vent, angling diagonally to allow his broad shoulders to fit, first one side and then the other. A second later his trim hips disappeared and finally his feet.

China held her breath and waited.

Sierra grabbed her arm and tugged. "What do we do now?"

"Wait?"

Someone must have noticed the extra activity in the cubicle, or perhaps they'd seen Rick shimmy into the ceiling vent above the suspended bedside curtains. A group of three nurses and an ER doctor gathered at the door.

"What's going on?" Dr. Weinstein asked.

Sierra was quick to spill the beans. "My patient was here one minute and then the next thing I knew after the aftershock he disappeared into the ceiling, so China got Rick and he went in after him and now we're waiting to see if he found him," Sierra babbled.

Chuckles erupted from the group and a few more people gathered nearby, while normal ER work was suspended for the unusual.

A minute later, Rick's black cross-training shoes re-appeared at the vent opening.

Everyone applauded as a familiar, cold voice broke in. "What, may I ask, is going on?"

A chill ran up China's spine when she turned to see Dr. Morell at the ER entrance. Wide-eyed, she snapped her head back and ignored him, concentrating instead on the scuffling and sliding overhead in the ceiling.

She heard Dr. Weinstein explain the situation to his colleague just as Rick dropped out of the ceiling, with Peter's foot safely attached to his hand.

"Come on, Peter. Everything's OK." Rick tugged on his shoe and another appeared. Soon two gangly legs hung from the ceiling. China steadied Rick by holding onto one of his knees, and Sierra held the other from the opposite side of the gurney. Slowly, the rest of Peter got pulled out of the vent and onto the hospital bed. For a second time the gathered group applauded, and this time even a few patients joined in.

A wild-eyed, frantic young psych patient got coaxed off the bed by Sierra. She offered him a drink of water and promised to stay by his side while he got the medical attention he needed.

"Give him a sedative while you're at it," Dr. Weinstein said, writing an order.

Rick smiled, his face dirty, as he dusted off his scrubs. China grinned back tensely, filled with apprehension, knowing who waited outside.

He clapped his hands together, raised and shook them in victory, like a heavyweight champion for the crowd. "Anything for the ER, folks."

"Rick?"

Recognition registered in his eyes at the sound of his father's voice. His jaw tightened, and he dropped his hands to his sides.

Dr. Morell gestured for Rick to join him on the other side of the nurses' station. "When you're through playing hero, I'd like a word with you," he said curtly.

Cringing with humiliation for Rick, China watched Dr. Morell walk toward the ER office. Rick took his time, made a wide sweep around the central station to where he'd left his white coat over the back of a chair. He carefully put it on and straightened the collar before joining his father.

China trotted across the ER to the medicine room to get a sedative for Sierra's patient so she wouldn't have to leave him alone, glad to have something to keep her busy. She jammed the key in the cupboard and slammed the medicine cups on the counter, hardly able to control her anger over the disrespect Dr. Morell had shown Rick in front of everyone. Next door, through the paper-thin walls, the conversation between Rick and his father heated up.

"What in the hell do you think we have security guards and the fire department for?"

"I know that guy from before. I knew he'd respond to me. And there wasn't a problem getting to him."

"Mercy Hospital could have wound up with two casualties, instead of one, with your shenanigans."

"If I thought for one moment I couldn't pull it off, I'd have been the first to call Security."

"We're liable for any injuries. This could have been a disaster."

"But it wasn't."

"You'll have to write up an incident report."

"I know the protocol."

"This type of careless behavior is the exact opposite of what the ER needs in a position of leadership."

"I disagree."

China heard the argumentative tone in Rick's voice. That was sure to raise Dr. Morell's hackles. During a brief silence she imagined the look on the doctor's face, cold, harder than ice, and hoped that Rick would stand his ground. When Dr. Morell spoke again, his harsh, controlled voice cut like a knife.

"Furthermore, and the main reason I came down here tonight, it has come to my policy and procedures committee's attention that you performed procedural sedation on an ER patient without benefit of medical doctor oversight."

"If it's the high school football player you're referring to, the patient was in pain. He was monitored. There were no complications."

"Our policy clearly states only a medical doctor can perform procedural sedation."

"I work under the doctor I'm assigned to in the ER on any given day."

"But Dr. Weinstein never signed the orders."

"Sometimes the patient needs to come before policy."

"Regardless of what you think, Rick, you don't write the rules around here. You follow them."

Dead silence.

Dr. Morell cleared his throat. "You may have blown your chance to become supervisor because of this."

Almost dizzy with rage, China couldn't contain herself any longer. Her quest to right the injustices of the world forced a reckless response. She walked around the corner, rapped on the office door and, without being asked, stepped inside.

"With all due respect, sir, in my opinion, what Rick did just now showed exemplary leadership." She shook with anger.

"And with all due respect, Ms. Seabury," Dr. Morell said, seething, "I am leery to take the opinion of any wanton woman who is involved with my son."

She wanted to fling herself at Dr. Morell and scratch out his eyes. She wanted to swear a blue streak. Instead, she stood statue-still, fighting off trembles. Using all her reserves, she worked to control her voice and her quivering lower lip. "You're not being fair."

Rick glared at his father, but offered nothing more in his defense.

"Let me tell you about fair, Ms. Seabury." Dr. Morell barely covered his contempt.

"Our argument has nothing to do with China—" Rick stepped forward.

"I think it does," Dr. Morell cut in. His stone-cold eyes glanced in calculated thought from Rick to China and back. "I plan on having an audit committee examine your figures for both the fundraiser and the high school event you've planned. Let's hope everything adds up." He huffed, and left the office.

Rick and China stood silent for several seconds, the room thick with tension. She wanted to console him, to tell him that now she realized what a bastard he had for a father. She wanted to rush into his arms and kiss away his pain.

Instead, an emotionless voice caught her off guard. "I don't know what you thought you were doing, but I don't need your help or pity." He brushed past her.

She followed him through the office door.

"I can take care of my own problems," he said, heading for the ER exit.

Fuming, she called after him. "Well, it didn't sound like you'd handled that one too well."

Realizing everyone in the entire ER was standing quietly, taking in every sentence, she bit her lip.

He stopped in mid-stride, and turned slowly. "In the future, China, if I need your help, I'll ask for it," he said with a cold stare reminiscent of his father's. "Until then stay out of my business."

The automatic door swung wide and, finally breaking eye contact, Rick left.

Stunned, China stood trembling. Her penchant for being rash had blown up in her face. She glanced around the ER where doctors, nurses and aides were busily working and pretending to mind their own business. Maybe they hadn't witnessed the blow-up.

Fat chance.

"What in heaven's name made you face off with Dr. Morell?" Sierra said, placing her arm around China's shoulders and guiding her to the nurses' lounge, bursting her bubble of hope that no one had noticed.

"I guess both Dr. Morell and Rick put me in my place." If she'd only thought it through, things might have been different. A sudden ache in her leg caused her to limp.

"I don't give a rip about Morell senior. Rick just doesn't want you fighting his battles—that's my take." Sierra handed her a cup of coffee.

"That was painfully clear."

OK. She'd been kicked in the teeth before. She could handle this. She rubbed her throbbing thigh and sat down.

"We're not even an item. Hell, we've only kissed a couple of times. What was I thinking?"

Sierra took a sip of her own coffee and leaned against the counter. "With the earthquake and all, you've been through a lot together. I think you bonded pretty quickly." A twinkle appeared in her eyes. "So how does he kiss?"

China rolled her eyes and moaned. "You have such a one-track mind."

"Maybe. But how does he kiss?"

She took a drink and thought about the ER resident playboy, the guy that every girl wanted a fling with. Why had he given her a chance at all? He seemed to genuinely like her, and she was just beginning to figure out how she felt about him. But then she had to go and ruin things by intruding in his personal battle with his dictator of a father. Sometimes she loathed the crusader-to-a-fault syndrome that ran her life. If she could only turn back the clock.

She remembered the soft look in his eyes when he'd first kissed her. And, yeah, the earth had moved. She'd felt that kiss down to her toes long before the earthquake had struck.

"How does he kiss?" China's eyes narrowed then softened. She sank back into one of the nursing lounge chairs and fought off a grin. "He kisses like a seismic event."

Rick stormed down the hall. The scene with his father and China had been too reminiscent of his mother coming to his rescue when he'd been a kid.

What do you mean, you didn't make the principles list? How come you're not taking more advance placement courses? What the hell is this "C" in chemistry? You mean to tell me that you're not planning to be a pre-med major in college?

His mother used to rush to his side and stand up for him against his overbearing, pompuous father.

Foolish as it was, by taking the PA job at Mercy Hospital after the army, he'd hoped to prove to his father, once and for all, that he deserved his respect. Well, he'd accomplished zip in two years, and the way he felt now, it might be a century before he ever earned his father's esteem.

Why even try?

He hadn't meant to bite China's head off, but she'd crossed over the line. The feud between father and son was none of her business.

Right now he didn't give a damn about where he was going. He took the elevator down a floor, pushed through the basement doors and outside to the parking lot. Anywhere was better than wherever his father was in that damned hospital.

Maybe it was time to find a job someplace else.

CHAPTER SEVEN

"THAT would be wonderful," China said, tucking the ER receiver between her chin and shoulder and writing down the date and time to meet with the police lieutenant. Maybe he'd be willing to be the master of ceremonies for the high school event. No harm in asking.

Oh, and she'd need a dozen volunteers to help pass fliers in the local neighborhoods, warning about the street closures for the carefully orchestrated car crash. She jotted that down.

Both the fire and police departments would be on hand to work out the logistics of the faked car crash the day before they filmed.

She'd agreed to work with the high school video class on filming the event to show to local schools. Hopefully it would drive home the point about the horrors of irresponsible teen driving.

Thank heavens she'd had a busy schedule to preoccupy her, instead of pining away for Rick the past two weeks. They'd avoided each other completely since the scene in the ER. And, of course, he hadn't called her once.

So why was he approaching her now?

Her knees went weak and her heart raced. She kept writing, but lost control of her hand and the words didn't make any sense.

"China?" He scratched his nose, looking sheepish.

Willing herself to act casual, she glanced quickly at him, and then away. "Hi. You need something?"

"Can we step outside a minute? I'd like to talk to you."

She tried not to notice Sierra's obvious stare from across the ER, even while she prayed that her legs would carry her.

China nodded and followed him, hoping desperately that an apology was in the offing. She'd missed him. Missed the opportunity to know him better.

He pushed the metal sensor for the automatic doors, and they swooshed across the rubber floor mat as they opened. His usual bravado in the ER had evolved to quiet humility over the last couple of weeks. Never was it more apparent than now.

Using every effort to control her gait, though her legs felt like overcooked noodles, she held her head high and forced her eyes straight ahead as she stepped outside.

He led her to a bench near the circular driveway at the entrance to Mercy Hospital and waited for her to sit. She expected him to join her but he stood beside the bench, surprising her. He pushed his hands inside the pockets of his white coat, where he kept his stethoscope. Lately, he'd been wearing the coat all the time.

He cleared his throat and stared down the driveway.

"I need your help," he said flatly, the muscle in his jaw twitching the tiniest bit.

Hiding her disappointment, she blinked, and waited.

"D'Wayne's been messing up again. He's drinking and hanging out with his old friends, and he recently got his driver's license."

She took a deep breath. "I see."

For the first time he turned and looked directly at her, a glimmer of hope in his eyes. "You do?"

So their conversation wasn't going to be about them. The realization stung, but she'd get over it. And besides, this was right up her street, a kid in distress who needed to get on board with her crusade. It might not be what she'd hoped for with Rick but, yeah, she'd take it. It was for the greater good.

But first Rick would have to pay.

"Of course I do." She checked to make sure her hair was tightly in place. "You can talk until you turn blue with teenagers, but it doesn't sink in. D'Wayne needs to see the damage firsthand."

He cocked his head.

"Can you convince him to come around on Saturday? I've got a job for him."

"I'll make sure of it." The tension left his eyes and his hands reappeared from his pockets. He made a fist into the other palm. "Do you need an extra hand?"

Never one to squander opportunity, she gave a curt smile. "I'm expecting it. I need you to be the MC again. I originally intended to ask the police lieutenant but decided he was too much of an authority figure. They'd never listen to him." Thinking out loud, she scratched her head. "You have a natural way with teens." She avoided stating the obvious—the girls would go gaga. "I could definitely use your help."

His shoulders squared, he faced her, looking thoughtful. "Whatever you need. I'm there."

"Good." She stood, preparing to leave. Though she wasn't completely sure she deserved a shot at him, her fantasy of knowing Rick on a deep and personal level would have to be put on hold. Maybe it was for the best. It was definitely safer.

"China?"

She pulled out of her thoughts. "Yes?"

"You're letting your bangs grow out?"

"Oh, that look was so last week. Been there, done that." Sounding cavalier, she brushed the air with her hand.

"I liked that look."

Flustered, she checked her French twist again for any stray hairs. Off balance, she tried not to stumble when she stood up and Rick walked her back to the ER.

Saturday morning, China stood before the mirror, scissors in hand. "Here goes," she said, puffing out air. She took the first snip, practically closing her eyes. She snipped again, and again, until she'd reached the other side of her bangs. She brushed and blew off the extra hair, and took a step back.

Not bad.

Making another snap decision, today she'd wear her hair down. As though having a mind of its own, her hand reached for an eye-shadow compact, followed by some blush.

The clipboard was tight with notes. China didn't want to forget anything, but her mind couldn't focus. The front section of the high school bleachers was scattered with the volunteer teens in various stages of waking up. It was nine-fifteen. Where were Rick and D'Wayne?

A police officer explained how things would work. "Our goal is to realistically portray a fatal car accident. Two upper classmen will be chosen to play the drivers. One will die and one will survive. We will follow the events from the initial crash to the hospital and then to the morgue. Nothing drives the point home stronger than a touch of reality." He grimly scanned the teenagers with his scare-'em-straight stare. "Ms. Seabury?"

Fervently engrossed, China jumped to her feet just as Rick and D'Wayne turned the corner to the bleachers. Trying not to look distracted, she said, "I have arranged for a special person to speak next Tuesday, after the entire school has seen the video." Her eyes ran across the bleachers. "She's a teenager like you guys, but she happens to be famous."

"Who is she?" one of the girls called out.

"Be sure to come to the event and find out. Now, who is on the flyer committee?" A gothic-looking girl and a frighteningly thin guy raised their hands. "I have a list of names for you." She handed them a stack of papers. "These need to be distributed throughout the local neighborhoods that will be affected by our video shoot. Each person has been assigned a street to pass them out to."

Rick and D'Wayne took a seat.

"Who is on the video team?" Three other teens raised their hands. D'Wayne's hand shot up, too. "Have you signed up, D'Wayne?"

"Nah, but I want to."

She glanced at Rick. He nodded. "OK, I'll see what I can do."

"You have to be in the video class to take part," one of the other students said.

A carefully guarded look of disappointment covered D'Wayne's normally expressionless face.

"The video team will be under my direction. I'm sure I can find something for you to do." She returned her gaze to the bleachers. "We'll use two cameras and then we have a tight deadline to edit the tapes in time for viewing the next day. It will be grueling and long and I need your parents' consent to participate because we may be up half the night editing to meet our goal." She handed the forms out.

The high school principal walked up beside her. "We drew names for both of the drivers from those who volunteered. We'll announce them on Monday at the lunchtime rally."

"OK," China decided to wrap the meeting up. "It looks like things are moving along as we've planned. The fire and police departments will shut down the intersection and move the wrecked cars into place on Monday, after school. I'd like to do some pre-event filming this afternoon. Can any of you stick around?"

D'Wayne's hand shot up, but no one else's.

"Great. We'll line up our pre-accident driving shots today."

Rick smiled, and she knew she'd made the right decision.

Two hours later, after a long conversation on artistic vision, D'Wayne had a huge smile on his face. A natural at using a video camera, he'd convinced Rick to drive while he sat in the back seat and shot video footage over his shoulder.

"Swerve," D'Wayne said.

Rick did what he was told, but only after making sure it was safe.

"Good. Now do it again."

China laughed, and covered her mouth.

D'Wayne focused the camera on China. "No, that's good. Keep laughing. We'll keep it in the video, like you're partying in the car."

Proud of his teenage charge, Rick shot a grin toward China. "Who the heck is that kid?" He glanced playfully toward the back seat. "The president of Future Directors of America?"

"Dawg, just do what I say." D'Wayne faked annoyance, and stayed on task. "Laugh China. Now swerve, Rick."

A few swerves later, Rick sensed something was wrong. China looked tense. She held onto the armrest with white knuckles, and her foot kept reaching for an imaginary brake.

"That's a wrap," Rick said. "Speaking of wrap, who's up for lunch? I'm hungry."

"I heard that," D'Wayne said.

"Does that mean you're hungry, too?"

"Let's eat, Dawg."

"Well I don't know about you guys." China spoke up for the first time in several minutes. "But I'm certainly not eating any dog."

D'Wayne made an exasperated sound, but grinned wide. "That's whack, China."

She coughed into her hand. "Sorry."

How cute was that? Rick glanced at China. Her hair was down and her bangs were short again. So, she'd listened to him. Her green eyes sparkled in the afternoon sun and, best of all, she wore a snug polo shirt and tight jeans, revealing curves in all the right places. He remembered feeling those curves and wanting to explore further when they'd napped together in the cafeteria, but that was a thought for another time, hopefully one that would come to fruition.

And as usual she was a total dynamo, organizing such a big important event. Bottom line? She impressed the hell out of him.

And he'd missed her—that was for sure.

After the scene with his father, he'd felt humiliated. China had tried to rescue him and, well, hell, he was a grown man, he hadn't needed rescuing, and his pride had taken over. He'd missed out on two weeks of getting to know China better. Yes, it had been a stupid thing to do, but he'd shut her out, and now it was time to make up for it.

He drove to a restaurant and parked the car. D'Wayne hopped out at lightning speed.

"After we eat, and I drive D'Wayne home, why don't we talk about how we want to film the emergency room scene, and what you want me to say at the assembly? I'm sure you've already worked out the logistics, but Chloe and Jezebel would love to see you again, and I could make a pot of coffee."

She lifted her splendid dark brows, which almost touched her newly trimmed bangs, and her mouth twitched at one corner.

D'Wayne's face appeared at the open passenger window. "Look out, China. He's straight up puttin' the moves on you."

China was amazed how back to normal things looked at Rick's house compared to after the earthquake had hit.

Jezebel and Chloe danced around her legs, rubbing up against her and sniffing her hands, fishing for a pat on the head. She bent down to greet each of them, nose to nose.

She glanced up, and her eyes met Rick's. After a lazy, appreciative stare, he cleared his throat.

"Would you rather have some lemonade or iced tea? How about both? I've heard they're pretty good mixed together."

Was it her imagination, or did Rick sound nervous? If anyone should be nervous, it should be her. She'd thought about him every day since their argument, and had planned how she'd replay the whole scene if given the chance. Maybe now, however, it was better just to move on and be done with whatever bad blood ran between Rick and his father. If they hadn't resolved their rift in thirty years, what in heaven's name had made her think she could?

"Actually, Rick, you put the thought of coffee in my head, so I'll hold you to it. Is that OK?" She ran her fingertips nervously through the hair at her neck. His eyes followed her hand.

He'd put a few other thoughts into her head that she'd like to hold him to, as well, but she knew that would never happen. She'd never let it.

Looking relieved with having an assigned task, he pushed the kitchen door open. Chloe and Jezebel pranced through. "Why don't you keep me company? I've got more of those chocolate cookies."

China grinned and followed him into the kitchen. A chill coursed up her spine. He didn't need to bribe her with cookies.

When he opened the cupboard door, she enjoyed the sight of his broad shoulders and tight, narrow hips when he bent over and reached inside for the coffee. Tingles trickled from her head across her shoulders at the sight of him. Her goofy picture, placed in a position of prominence on his refrigerator, almost jolted her out of her amorous mood.

He looked over his shoulder and gave a thoughtful smile before continuing his search. He stopped what he was doing, as though having a change of heart, and closed the door without the coffee. Had he read her mind? He shifted and stared at her with fire in his eyes.

"To hell with the coffee," he said, rushing to her and gathering her into his strong embrace.

She melted into his arms and wrapped hers around his neck to keep from losing her balance. The tingles had turned to electric shivers all the way down to her toes.

He kissed her hard, like a starving man finding sustenance. And she eagerly joined him in the feeding frenzy. His hot breath cut across her face. She recaptured his lips and closed her eyes, holding him tight at his neck, savoring his rock-like shoulders. She inhaled deeply, remembering his special aroma: sandalwood and testosterone. And every cell in her body reacted to him, begging for attention.

His hot kisses traveled to her neck, making her knees grow weak, and a foreign, almost forgotten warmth awakened in her core. She wanted him.

He leaned her against the wall and devoured her mouth. His hand glided up from hip to waist to flank. He hesitated a millisecond before cupping her breast. She pushed into his touch, wanting more, wishing the polo shirt and bra would disappear. Her breasts tingled and tightened under his attention. He ran his thumb lightly across her pebbled nipple, forcing it even tighter. Oh, why did they have to have clothes on?

Her leg wrapped around his thigh and he leaned in even closer. His large, strong hand explored her bottom before pulling her closer.

Wet between the legs, she pressed against the firm bulge in his jeans, searching for satisfaction.

He groaned.

Panting and whining and a fuzzy head pushed and nudged their knees. Rick stopped the kiss. China looked down at two sets of black eyes curiously watching them, and she giggled with relief.

Her hand flew to her mouth. "I'm sorry, but I forgot we had an audience."

Rick scrubbed his face and ran his hand through his hair. "Chloe? Can't you see I'm busy?" He nudged the dog away with his boot. "Go outside."

Jezebel yipped.

"Get. Both of you." He shook his head, gave China one quick nip to the neck, and grinned. "Now, where were we?"

The brief break in passion allowed an old and penitent friend to slide in. Guilt. Though she wanted to run, she wanted Rick more than she'd wanted anything in years. But did she deserve him? Resigned to bow down to her ever-present demons, she thought fast.

"Talk about a mood-breaker," she said, pulling back and straightening her top.

This was the closest she'd come to making love in years, and goose-bumps traveled across her skin at the thought. She sighed and quelled the urge to jump his bones, dogs or no dogs. Then she remembered the flaws that would keep her from ever allowing a man close again, and she took a cold mental shower.

Her fingers glided across her hair, primly straightening it. She stiffened her shoulders and embraced her resolve to stay on track.

"We do have work to do," she said. She opened the refrigerator door, surveying its contents, finally finding the coffee and releasing a strong whoosh of cool air.

China grinned when D'Wayne grimaced while the finishing touches to the gashing, deep head wound were made on him. Staring into a mirror, he looked dizzy at the sight of his fake blood, bone, and exposed tissues.

"Man," he said. "It looks for real."

Thanks to Brianna Cummings's participation in the teen driving awareness program, she'd made the make-up artist from her popular television show available. The TV writers had cleverly turned her into a zombie. The producer had agreed to make her one of the "living dead" for the rest of the season. Brianna was available for voiceovers, and the director used the actress's stand-in on the set while she healed. The writers promised to work the transformation out as some miracle on the show by next year. In the meantime, she and her plastic surgeon had a few miracles to work out themselves.

"Wow. This is bangin', dude," D'Wayne said to the man. "I look like I've had a bad accident, like a hatchet hit my head or something." He covered his mouth and laughed.

"Yeah?" the man answered. "Well, you're supposed to be dead."

"And he is." China stepped up. "Come on, D'Wayne, your wreck is waiting."

She grabbed his hand and led him to the carnage of the pre-planned vehicle accident at a neighborhood intersection.

A fireman met them and showed D'Wayne how to crawl inside. "We'll pretend to use the jaws of life on you for the film."

OK, so China had had to pull some strings to get D'Wayne's name chosen for the dead teen role, but it was well worth it. According to Rick, he'd been drinking with friends. If she could prevent him from ever driving while under the influence by showing him the possible consequences, she'd have done more than she'd ever hoped with her personal crusade.

"One teen at a time" had become her slogan, and D'Wayne was next in line.

Using her megaphone, China rattled off directions to the participants. The police officers had the streets cordoned off; the fire department and emergency medical technicians were ready and waiting with the ambulance; the teen playing the drunk-driving role prepared to fail the roadside sobriety test; and the cameras were ready to roll.

"Action," China yelled, feeling all-powerful.

As planned, the video squad filmed the sequence. The fire truck siren blared as the emergency services descended on the make-believe accident. Controlled chaos ensued, exactly as they'd rehearsed. The drunken teen got handcuffed and taken away in the police car, and the jaws of life removed the driver's door in order to rescue D'Wayne. He was placed on a gurney and rolled into an ambulance. A hearse was parked next to it for dramatic effect.

One video camera followed the drunken teenager through his processing at the police department, and the other camera followed D'Wayne to the ER.

Rick starred in the mock code blue emergency room scene later that afternoon. D'Wayne lay still on the ER bed as half a dozen hospital workers gathered around.

"Put him on the monitor," Rick said. "He's lost a lot of blood. Get a line in, normal saline, wide open." He hooked D'Wayne up to an automatic blood-pressure machine. "Stat type and cross-match."

The other ER employees hustled about looking busy, pretending to run the near code as usual in a blur of blue and green scrubs, masks, goggles, and gloves. A student dressed in a black robe with a hood hovered in the background.

"He's bottoming out. B/P's 80 over 30. Hang a liter of plasmanate."

They'd rigged the monitor to trigger its high-pitched alarm, which rent the air.

"Straight line. Zap him! Two hundred joules. All clear? Fire. Draw up some epi."

China saw D'Wayne peek from under his tight-pinched eyelids from time to time, an anxious look on his face.

Good. I hope we scare his baggy-jeans ass off.

Later, Rick dramatically pulled the sheet over D'Wayne's face, and another student filmed as a hooded figure placed the nametag on his big toe. It read: "Deceased. John Doe."

Rick had talked D'Wayne's mother into being in the video. A natural actress, she broke down in tears when Rick told her that her son had died.

"My baby," she gasped. "Oh, God, no! My boy."

She collapsed into Rick's arms, sending a chill up China's spine. How had her best friend Amy's mother reacted when she'd gotten the word ten years ago?

Refusing to be thrown off track, China concentrated on the job at hand, and pushed nightmarish memories to the back of her mind.

By three in the morning, China and the video class had finished editing the twenty-minute film, complete with music and voiceovers by Rick. She carried the finished film home as if it were gold, collapsed onto her bed, and tucked it under her pillow for safekeeping. Then she passed out from exhaustion with a smile of satisfaction on her face.

"We're here today—" Rick stood on the high school auditorium stage on Tuesday afternoon in black jeans and matching T-shirt "—to honor 31,000 teens who have died over the past decade from car crashes." He waited for the chattering to die down before he continued. "Every year, more and more of you…" he dramatically pointed to the audience "…will die from either driving, being a passenger in a car with a teen driver, or being in an accident caused by a teen driver." He cleared his throat and scanned the now-silent crowd. "Alcohol, drugs, loud music, distracting friends, cellphones. The list of excuses goes on and on, but unfortunately the grim reaper doesn't care what your reason is. He just wants someone new to keep him company."

On cue, the tallest basketball player they'd been able to find from the team stepped onto the stage in a black cape with a hood, his face painted ghoulish white and carrying a scythe. An imposing Halloween-type figure, he jumped into the audience and randomly chose a student, dragged him onto the stage and delivered him to Rick.

China watched with delight as a girl screamed and the audience gasped when the dark figure snatched up one of them. She prayed the program would get through to someone today. It was her personal hope for redemption. Her long, unanswered prayer.

Rick nodded solemnly at the victim.

"What's your name?"

"Arturo Hernandez."

"Follow me, Arturo." Rick took hold of his elbow. "We're going for a ride."

The lights dimmed and the video started with the sound of laughter and rap music and a teenager behind the wheel of a car.

Twenty minutes later, when the video ended, the somber crowd remained silent.

"I'd like to introduce our special guest," Rick said, returning to the stage. "A courageous young woman you all know from the hit television series, *The Undead*. You may know her as Zola, but Hollywood knows her as Brianna Cummings!"

The audience went wild.

"I have a confession to make," Brianna began, when the audience finally settled down. "I used to smoke. I knew I shouldn't, but I did. I mean, I know about lung cancer, but I never dreamed smoking could cause me to have a car accident and almost kill me."

Fresh pink scars lined her cheek and forehead. Her nose had been straightened, but now looked bumpy and swollen compared to its prior perfection.

With her permission, a picture of her was flashed on a screen, fresh from the ER two months earlier. She was covered with stitches and dressings, her nose was bent out of shape, her lips were bloody and swollen, and there was bruising under both of her eyes.

She glanced at it, and back to the students. "I'm lucky to be alive. How did my Corvette get wrapped around a pole, you ask? Contrary to rumor, it didn't involve drugs or alcohol. No. I had a life-threatening accident because I was talking on a cellphone and trying to light a cigarette while speeding down Sunset Boulevard. I thought I could do it all. Turns out I was wrong. I know we live in the world of multi-tasking, but I've learned when we're driving, that's the only thing we should be doing."

From backstage China peeked out and caught a glimpse of D'Wayne raptly watching the young actress. Intense satisfaction caused her to inhale raggedly. A firm hand cupped her elbow.

"This is going great," Rick whispered.

She nodded and looked over her shoulder at him.

"I think you're changing lives today, China. You can be proud."

Without warning the floodgates of her soul opened up and she wept uncontrollably. He guided her into his chest, wrapped her up in a comforting embrace and rocked her.

"I don't know what's haunting you, honey, but you're working miracles here today."

He cupped her face with his hands and stared at her. She wiped her cheeks with the cuffs of her sleeves.

"Look out there." He turned her head. "They're listening. You're saving lives." He kissed her forehead and snuggled her back into his arms. "You've made a difference."

She believed him. The sincerity in his voice made her skin prickle. She let herself dream for a brief moment, and imagined a chance for a normal life with a guy like Rick. In the center of her heart, she felt a kernel of love sprout.

"Let's celebrate this weekend with that special dinner date I purchased." He nuzzled her cheek. "I'll arrange everything. All you have to do is show up. What do you say?"

She glanced quickly into his eyes.

"Come on, honey. You deserve it."

She gave a hesitant, unconvincing nod.

How would he feel about her if she told him her deepest secret? If he knew the truth about her past, how she'd messed up and taken the life of her best friend. If Rick knew the whole story, would he still call her honey?

CHAPTER EIGHT

CHINA opened the door on Friday night to find Rick leaning against the frame. Thick brown hair, still damp from a recent shower, curled gently at his neck. He was wearing a silky thin button-up shirt, which he hadn't tucked in, beneath a pinstriped jacket. Faded, tight jeans and his signature cowboy boots rounded out the near perfect picture.

She wavered on her high heels.

He felt too close. Looking more like a fire department calendar pin-up than her date, she wanted to back up and run for the hills.

"You look great," he said.

Ditto.

His gaze drifted from her face down to her feet. A big smile stretched across his cheeks and he lifted his brows. "And you wore my favorite shoes."

A blanket of heat covered her entire body under his intense scrutiny. She felt daring enough, wearing the glove-tight black leather pants and high-heeled sandals. Obviously he had been hoping for a mini-skirt. But didn't the nearly see-through black lace top and matching bra make up for it?

"Would you like to come in?" Nervous hands flitted from her neck to her waist.

He reached for her wrist, tugged her close and dropped a light kiss on the corner of her mouth. Tingles fanned across her shoulders.

"Ask me that again later," he said. "If I come inside now, we may never make it out in time for our dinner reservations."

What was she going to do with him? Every time he came around she fell apart. One look, one touch and she developed an out-of-body experience, leaving her weak at the knees and foggy-minded.

"Oh. OK," she said, forcing a quick recovery. "Let me get my purse."

She'd taken great care in preparing for tonight. Using her tropical magic shampoo, special plumeria body lotion, and an extra dab or two of make-up when she'd gotten ready, she'd wondered what her intentions were for the evening. Truth was, she hadn't wanted to impress a man this much since the night she'd known she would become engaged, three and a half years ago.

She didn't just want Rick Morell. Crazy as it seemed in such a short period of time, she thought she'd fallen in love with him. He'd proved his sincerity and worth over and over to her in the last few weeks, and she'd succumbed to his natural charm. But it was more than physical, that much she knew. He'd also managed to touch a part of her she'd kept buried. He made her feel lovable again. And realizing he wasn't as perfect as he seemed made him all the more appealing.

Was she sure she was ready for the next step?

When she got back to the door, Rick cast her a mischievous glance and asked, "Are you ready?"

This time China had been the one to ask Sierra to switch shifts with her at work, even going so far as to offer to pay for a sitter for Timmy since it was Friday night and Lance's bowling night. There was no way she'd miss her auction-bought celebration date with Rick for anything in the world. The odd thing was, she almost felt she deserved it. Funny how a few weeks could make such a big difference in a person's outlook on life.

China closed the door and made an effort to focus on small talk. "How did your job interview go today?"

Rick's smile spread to a grin. "They asked all the right questions and I gave all the right answers."

Hating to put a dampener on his mood, she hesitated before asking, "Was your father on the panel?"

He tossed his head and walked jauntily down her steps toward his car. "Nope."

"Well, whew," she said when he opened the door for her. "That must have made your day." She smiled and slipped inside.

Rick leaned over. "Conflict of interest, they said." He laughed. "Little did they know it worked in my favor."

Over dinner, Rick couldn't quit looking at China. She glowed with pride, but something more sparkled in her eyes, something intentional and alluring. He hoped he was the reason for that special look. He'd realized while getting ready for their date that the feelings he had for China went beyond infatuation. Hell, he'd almost tripped in the shower when the thought had hit him between the eyes. He loved her. Now all he needed was a way to find the right time to tell her.

The beachfront restaurant was crowded and noisy, but the view of the ocean from their reserved table was phenomenal, and he wanted to impress China tonight. When was the last time he'd gone to the effort of really working for a woman? He had to admit it was exciting and fun.

By the sexy way she'd dressed, he had high hopes she wanted to impress him, too. And so far she was doing a fantastic job. As long as he could keep her from pulling her usual disappearing act, the one where they'd reach a new level of closeness and she'd withdraw, like she'd done since Tuesday after the high school video program, he had a fighting chance.

When he'd gotten a glance earlier at how the second-flesh leather slacks caressed her shapely hips and rear end, he'd almost stumbled down the steps. Now, if he could only keep from drooling, he might have a shot at getting to third base tonight. And if he got really lucky, he might make it to home plate. He delved into his meal with gusto. A guy could dream, couldn't he?

A long silence pressured him to make small talk. He cleared his throat. "I heard they had an 80 per cent success rate for signing the safe driving agreement from those students attending the assembly," he said, trying to make her think his head was somewhere besides the bedroom.

She used her napkin to daintily wipe her mouth. "My stats showed 87 per cent."

True to form, she'd corrected him. Never mess with a crusader's statistics. He fought off a smile.

He loved it when she got prim. She tossed her silky black hair over her shoulder and challenged him with forest-deep eyes from under those sexy bangs. Oh, yeah, she was proud, and it turned him on. But what about China didn't excite him?

"And D'Wayne was the first one to sign it. Isn't that great?" She beamed.

He nodded. "I'm positive we've turned him around." He grinned. "I think the point really got driven home when we put him in a body bag, zipped it up and slid him into the fridge in the morgue. Little did he know the video camera wasn't even running then."

They laughed, and he thought he caught a glimpse of adoration on her face. Now, that was progress. He liked making her smile. In his opinion, she didn't do it nearly enough. His heart had ached for her on Tuesday when she'd fallen apart. Hell, he'd wished he could take away her pain. But like a brave little soldier, she always kept up her guard.

She'd recovered from her tears in record time and wriggled free from his embrace, once again ready to take the lead in her project. As if closing an iron gate, she'd willed her emotions to be locked away. If he could only break through the barrier she hid behind. Come out, China. Let's finally get to know each other. Let me into your life.

He knew they had a lot in common and Lord only knew how strong the sexual attraction was, at least on his part. But she couldn't fool him. Every time they'd kissed, a powerful surge of desire had ignited, and she'd been right there with him. He could feel it—they were special together. He knew it was love. But now wasn't

the time to think about that, or he'd never make it
through dinner.

Now, where were they? Right. D'Wayne and the
assembly agreement.

Rick watched her animated recounting of the recent
triumph. He could relate to how she must feel about
being successful. He remembered feeling proud in the
service when three-quarters of the men he'd tended in
combat had progressed without complications. Field
medicine was a challenge, to be sure, but the biggest
enemy would always be infection, and if he could
prevent it, he'd done his job. Yeah, he knew about
success and self-satisfaction.

He clicked back into their conversation.

"I couldn't wait to share the good news with Mercy
Hospital. I even pitched my next project to them, and
they're already on board." She sipped her water. "And
then, of course, I called my mom. She's my biggest
fan."

A guarded expression accompanied China's abrupt
stop, as though she worried she'd said something
wrong.

He'd long ago given up sharing any good news
with his old man, if that was what she was concerned
about. No point.

"Your mother has a lot to be proud of in you."

Her hand darted to his arm. "Your father does, too.
Maybe one day he'll figure that out."

Oh, no. He didn't want tonight to turn into a pity
party. Not on the night when he'd decided to tell China
how he truly felt about her. He'd change the subject, and
quick.

"Let's drink a toast." He raised his glass of deep red wine. "To your success, and all the good you bring into the world."

Instead of lightening the mood, a veil of sadness covered China's previously glowing face. She tried to hide it, but it was as apparent as the pale half-moon-shaped scar on her brow.

They solemnly clicked glasses and sipped. He saw her thick lashes flutter and troubled thoughts cross her face. He'd pushed too hard, and now he was losing her, damn it. After their toast he leaned in, reached for her hand, and searched her eyes. What was she not telling him?

What would he think of her when he found out about her past, about what she had done?

China couldn't tolerate another moment of smolder-ing looks from Rick. Her tingle-scale had risen to seismic proportions with each attentive touch. When he reached across the table and took her hand, her heart almost imploded. And the crazy thing was, he didn't have anything in particular to say. He just probed with his stare, gazing into her eyes with yet another moony grin like a man in love, like a man who really wanted to know all about her, which only made her more uncomfortable.

She didn't deserve anyone's love or respect.

She squirmed in her chair.

If he kept on giving her those sexy lover's looks, she'd be sitting in a pool of sweat—not very appealing.

The sudden need to freshen up had her gingerly removing her hand from under his.

"I need a quick trip to the ladies' room," she said, with a nervous quiver in her voice.

He smiled and nodded knowingly, releasing her. Though she was sure a slight look of disappointment registered in his penetrating eyes when she stood.

When she walked away, she used every fiber of control to appear composed. And she did fine until she passed the bar, her gaze scanning the crowd, and a strikingly familiar face smiled at her.

China stumbled on the carpet, catching the back of a barstool to help recover her balance.

The girl looked just like Amy.

She broke into a cold sweat and strode to the powder room to regroup.

Shaky hands reached for her mouth, then touched her cheek and adjusted her hair. She primped and prayed that her speeding heartbeat would return to normal.

It was just her imagination.

Old guilt-ridden feelings strangled the joy and wonder at rediscovering love with Rick. No. She didn't deserve happiness—hadn't that familiar face at the bar been a sign?

China tried to recover a semblance of control. As she stepped up to the basin, the bathroom door opened. The same young woman from the bar burst unsteadily into the room. She'd obviously been drinking. Up close she looked younger than Amy would have been. China attempted to stay calm, and worked to steady her chaotic breathing while she washed her hands.

Her mind was playing tricks on her. That's all.

The tipsy woman grinned widely and looked straight at China. "Hi, there," she said breezily. "You have a great life. OK? You deserve it, sweetie." She giggled. "Hell, we all do."

We all do.

Something in China broke free. The emotional hand-cuffs she'd been bound to for years suddenly released their hold. Gooseflesh covered her body.

She deserved to be happy.

She wanted to weep, but stopped herself. She looked toward the ceiling and smiled. Feeling buoy-ant and free for the first time she could remember since high school, she dashed out of the ladies' room, eager and excited to get back to Rick. Onward across the hard wood floor, she almost collided with a couple dancing.

She grabbed the man's arm and apologized. "I'm sorry. I get klutzy when I fall in love."

The female partner nodded with a knowing look, and China, feeling like a brand-new woman, strode back to the table where Rick, the man she loved, waited.

China came bounding toward the table a different woman than the one that'd left, smiling bright as the planet Venus. Things were definitely looking up, and hopefully in his favor. After all, Venus was the goddess of love. Rick was glad he'd already paid the bill.

He stood in anticipation to greet her. "Shall we go?"

She tossed him a winsome glance. "Your place or mine?"

Now, that was a welcome change, and all the encour-agement he needed. He laced his fingers through hers and led her out to the parking lot at a vigorous pace. Liquid heat flowed up his arm and into his chest, setting his soul on fire as they walked. The damp sea air couldn't cool him down. No. Only one person could do that, but first it was sure as hell going to get a lot hotter.

They reached the car parked in the far corner of the dimly lit lot in record time. He couldn't control himself another second.

Instead of unlocking the car door, he backed China against it in a full body press. She smelled fruity and he expected her skin to taste sweet. He nipped her neck, soft and warm like honey. His mouth covered hers in a lusty, deep kiss.

Eager didn't begin to describe her pleasing response. Her arms moved in a whirlwind through his hair, across his neck, over his back, and along his hips when they kissed, as though she couldn't get enough of him. Her signal was loud and clear and it nearly drove him wild.

He ran his hands along her sides, searching for bare flesh. Her tight, sexy top co-operated and rose above her waist. The feel of hot, smooth skin sent him reeling. On a crazed whim of desire, he took off her top, leaving only her bra in place. She didn't seem to mind either.

Fully erect and pressing against her hips, he almost lost control and tried to back off, but she wouldn't let him. Her hands skittered across his shaft then cupped his hips and held him close.

He gazed down at the ample cleavage pressed against his shirt. All he could think of was how to rip off her clothes in a public parking lot without anyone else noticing.

Their messy, ravenous kisses could barely be controlled. She gasped for air. He dove into her neck and she moaned; her chest lifted and pushed against his. Beneath the lace bra her soft breasts felt like heaven and he needed more of her, right there and then.

He unclasped her waistband and plunged his hand inside, sliding into her barely-there underwear. She gasped and he kissed her quiet. He made a delicate search and found her slick and wet, then massaged her until she nearly swooned, completely under his spell.

Stretching the moment, he kissed her gently and lovingly, using his tongue to taunt and torture her earlobes and the supple flesh of her neck. She kissed him back with warm, pliant lips and quiet whimpers.

Rick couldn't keep his new-found secret another second. He pressed his forehead to hers and forced her to look at him. "China, I want you to know something," he said. "I've got to make you understand how much I'm in love with you."

Her eyes brightened with surprise, but she couldn't seem to speak. He knew he was completely in control, and to prove his love he planned to satisfy her and deny himself.

Never releasing the pressure below, he stared into her heavy-lidded gaze. He knew to respect the gift of her surrender. The frantic, heady moment in the parking lot could have seemed surreal, but it was special. And he wasn't having an incredibly hot and sexy moment in a parking lot with just any woman—it was with China, the woman he loved.

He kissed her again, she moaned and tensed, then groaned, opening her mouth for him to kiss and delve deeper. Following her lead, he buried his tongue inside, and she went frantic with the double excitement.

He brought her to her peak then backed off, calming her down with hot kisses, just so he could do it again. Over and over he carried her to the edge but slowed down to suspend the sublime pleasure until she practically begged him. Her leg wrapped around his hips, smashing him against his own hand. One final touch sent her whirling through the night.

She gasped. He covered her mouth so no one could hear her ecstatic outburst while she writhed beside him for several long moments.

He felt her rhythmic spasms of pleasure under his fingers and smiled, so pleased to give her what she'd long deserved, release from all her cares, if only for a moment.

When she'd calmed down, he removed his hand from inside her pants, and ran it across her waist up and under her bra to her breast, pleased to feel the tightly peaked skin. He smiled at her with a twinge of regret that their tryst was over and zipped up her pants. He searched for her blouse on the roof of the car and offered it to her.

She snapped it up, and looked into his eyes with heat and desire written in her stare. Before she put on the top, she planted a hot, wet kiss on his lips, and when she'd finished, in a commanding tone said, "My place. Your turn. Now."

After the greatest invitation in his lifetime, he couldn't open the car door quickly enough.

They barely made it inside her house before Rick's shirt and her bra were off. His large hands felt wonderful against her breasts. China arched into his grasp and he moaned with pleasure before taking her taut breast into his mouth.

She copied his moan in sheer pleasure. She explored the brick-hard muscles of his chest, lightly covered with curly brown hair, and marveled at his strength.

She walked backwards toward her bedroom, and Rick, following close behind, never lost touch with her skin. She skillfully and intentionally bypassed the light switch and guided him directly to her bed. He already knew how to undo her leather pants, and was immediately on task while she fell onto the bed. He grinned in the dark when he realized he had to remove her shoes before the pants could come off. Taking time to admire, caress, and kiss each foot, he drove her to distraction.

Were any places on her body not erogenous zones tonight?

"Come," she said, beckoning with her finger. "Come to me."

Rick danced on one foot and then the other while he removed his boots, staring down at her all the while, driving her insane with anticipation. He dove into his pocket for a small foil package. "I was hoping you might see things my way." He displayed the condom with a grin, as if a treasure, and stripped off his jeans. He covered her in naked perfection, his hands exploring every part of her before she had a chance to push the pillows out of the way.

Hard and long he pressed into her thigh and, still throbbing from earlier, she readily opened for him.

He slid on the condom and then into her in one heavenly move. It had been a long time since she'd made love. He noticed and took great care to be gentle.

The considerate gesture touched her soul. Turned on and longing to feel him deep inside, she adjusted to his size quickly. Every cell in her body prickled with excitement at his touch.

"You're perfect," he whispered.

They moved together in a dazed lovers' rhythm, kissing and groping, pressing and pushing, until they found the perfect tempo and spot. Chills shot through her body at lightning speed. Quaking with sublime sensitivity, every fiber tensed and ached for satisfaction.

His muscles stiffened like boards, and for one second he went perfectly still. He groaned and started up again, deeper and harder. She loved his extra-firm thrusts just before he came, and she quickly followed with a roller-coaster ride of gasps, thrills, spasms, and heavenly release.

Several moments later, they collapsed together in a puddle of satisfied flesh, feeling more like gelatin than flesh and bone.

"Hmm," he growled. "The earth definitely moved." He kissed her neck and flopped back onto the pillow.

She giggled at his corny joke, and marveled at the new feeling of carelessness. It felt wonderful to be back among the living and vibrant again.

A few moments later, after fondling and cooing and showering compliments on each other, Rick jumped off the bed.

"I'll be right back, honey. Don't even think about going anywhere," he said, and left the room.

China lay suspended in heaven, floating on a cloud, and must have drifted off to another place.

Had this really happened? Had she just made love with Rick Morell?

A bright flash forced her eyes open. She sat bolt upright. Rick had turned on the lights.

"Turn off the lights."

She scrambled for the sheets to cover her scarred and mangled legs, but it was too late. She saw the look on his face and it was horror-struck.

She withdrew, recognizing the expression. She repulsed him, just like she'd repulsed her ex-fiancé. The realization stabbed at her heart.

He stepped forward with a curious glance, like an eyewitness at an accident on the side of the road. "Let me see, China. What are you hiding?"

"No." She tightened the sheets around her.

"I felt your scars when we made love. Did you think I wouldn't?"

"At the time, I wasn't thinking at all."

"Come on, let me see," he said. "What horrible thing happened to you?"

Against her better judgement, she moved the sheet to expose herself.

Two years and five operations' worth of scars stretched across her thighs, knees and calves. Deep gashes of flesh, never to be restored, marred her legs. Metal rods, plates, pins and screws had replaced shattered bones and joints. Two years of rehab had helped her strengthen what muscle she had left, and had taught her how to walk almost like a normal person again. Every nightmare of the memory was on display for Rick to examine. There was nothing more to hide.

He sat on the edge of the bed and lightly traced one jagged, white gouging scar up to her thigh. A gentle yet intense look told her he was deeply moved by the extent of her injuries. His dark brown eyes studied her differently now, no longer like a woman he'd just made love to. Under his gaze, she felt more like a specimen.

"Oh, honey," he said, with a crack in his voice.

A moment ago she had been the goddess of his sexual desire, now she evoked only sympathy. No. She wouldn't stand for it. She couldn't bear it.

"I don't need your pity." Her voice quivered.

He shook his head. "I'm not offering it. It doesn't matter to me how your legs look. I don't care."

"Oh, yes, you do care. Remember how quick you were to write off Brianna Cummings? Oh, and don't forget the football player?" She snapped her fingers. "Just like that, you closed the door on their careers and didn't even look back."

"What happens in the ER stays in the ER. That's a different world, and you know it. It's part of the survival techniques we all use to get by. Otherwise we'd all go crazy. Cut me some slack here, China. I'm just trying to comprehend the burden you've been carrying around."

"You can't tell me my scars don't turn you off. You said it yourself, 'Life's all about appearances.' I just heard you say, 'What horrible thing happened to you?' I'm damaged goods and you can't accept anything but perfection."

Her insult hit home. He rose from the bed with a shuttered glare. "Actually," he said laconically, "it's my father who can't accept anything but perfection. As far as I can tell, the only person around here who can't accept your scars is you."

She pulled the covers closer to her chin.

"Didn't you hear me when I said I love you?" Anger colored the words that had sent her reeling earlier. "Because that hasn't changed."

She shook her head, not believing a word he said.

"Don't you think I noticed that you limp sometimes at work? That you always wear slacks or long skirts? I may be a guy, but I could tell you always pushed people away, and I couldn't understand why. OK, so your legs are messed up. So what? You're beautiful to me."

He sat on the bed beside her. She turned away.

"So what?" He had no idea what dealing with her legs was like. The shame. The pain. The guilt. "You don't understand."

He reached for her hand, but she pulled it away. "Look, I can't know the pain you've been through, but you can walk now, and you don't seem to be in pain every second. Hell, you gave no sign of pain when we made love. Maybe it's time to accept what's happened to you, quit hiding, and move on."

Humility and anger had taken hold. The nerve of him to lecture her. How could he pretend to still love her after seeing her legs? It was too late. She'd seen his face. He'd be no different than her ex-fiancé, and some time in the future, when it was OK to drop her, he would, without looking like a bad guy.

"Acceptance?" He was telling her to move on? She knew the drill—been there, done that. She'd learned her lesson and would protect herself at all costs. A whirlwind of confusion swept across her mind and she struck out.

"You want to talk about acceptance?" she said. "You can't act all high and mighty. Until you learn to stand up to that ogre of a father, you'll never be able to accept or respect yourself. And until then you'll never be a real man."

She'd hit below the belt, but she didn't care. He deserved her wrath, just for feeling sorry for her. She'd seen his face. How could she ever look at him again knowing he felt pity for her?

It didn't matter that he might have felt the same way when she'd rushed to his aid against his father. His scars were emotional; hers were real. He could change his circumstances.

"This isn't going to work out."

"China, listen to me. I don't care about your scars."

"This was a mistake. I should never have let this happen." Sign or no sign. "You need to leave."

Cold silence filled the room. Rick put his pants on and grabbed his shirt, preparing to leave. "You're not the only person in the world with hidden scars. And until you can accept yourself, you'll never be able to trust anyone, and you'll always be alone."

If she could have disappeared, she would have, but at that moment horrible flashes of another time and place flickered through her mind.

"You can't spend your whole life hiding from people and feelings," he said, but his voice sounded strangely distant.

She curled into a fetal ball and prayed the recurring flashback nightmare would go away.

"China. What's wrong?"

China giggled and danced behind the steering-wheel. How could anyone sit still when Smash Mouth sang "Walking on the Sun"? Amy sat shotgun, clapping her hands to the beat. This was the carefree life of a teenager, and it rocked. China glanced over with a huge grin, cutting a dance move in the air and snapping her fingers. "Look, Ma, no hands."

Amy wasn't smiling. Instead, terror flashed in her eyes as she looked ahead. China glanced back to the road in time to see an SUV barreling toward her. In an instant she'd crossed the dividing line on the two-way coastal road.

A horn honked loud and long, like a train going through a tunnel. She tried to swerve back to her lane, but her hands froze in place. She couldn't move or make a sound.

Her vision shut down.

A cacophony of screams and horns, and a sound she'd never forget from her friend until the day she died, preceded the inevitable head-on collision of metal wrenching metal as she slid under the dashboard and finally let out a blood-curdling scream.

China woke up to find Sierra sitting at her bedside with worry deeply written on her face.

"Hey, kid," she said. "It's been a long time since you've had one of your spells. How are you feeling?"

As China's eyes adjusted, she noticed her mother in the background. She quickly checked under the sheets to see if she was dressed. Someone had put her in pajamas and straightened the covers.

"Hi, baby." Her mother approached and sat on the other side of the bed, making it lopsided with her full-figured weight. "Are you better now? I'm going to stay the night with you in case you have your night terrors again."

"How did you get here?"

"Rick called," Sierra said. "He was worried about you. He said you were sick and he didn't want to leave you alone. He said he'd wait until I got here."

He couldn't have stuck around?

The bedside clock read 2 a.m. Her heart sank to her stomach where a queasy feeling took hold. He'd left her, just as she'd predicted. Maybe she would get sick again.

"Oh, right." She settled back on the bed, hiding her disappointment. She fluffed her pillow, but wanted to beat the living daylights out of it. "I guess when the going gets tough, Rick Morell gets going."

CHAPTER NINE

THE next day, Rick showed up to work clenching his jaw in full military don't-ask-and-I-won't-tell mode. WHAT the hell else was he supposed to do but suck it up?

He'd thought China had been having a seizure the night before, and he'd stayed close by her side, protecting her head, trying to calm her down. She'd slipped into another level of consciousness, and it had scared him more than combat.

The feeling of helplessness had been what he'd really been unable to handle. There hadn't seemed to be anything he could do for her. Once she'd passed out or calmed down or whatever the hell it had been, he'd checked her pulse to make sure she was OK. He'd washed her face and combed her hair, dressed her in her most conservative pajamas, then called Sierra.

Big sister had seemed to know exactly what he was talking about, and had promised to be right over. He'd sat stroking China's hair and holding her hand until she'd arrived. Never in his life had he hurt for someone else as much as he had for China. She didn't deserve to suffer like that. If he could've taken away her pain, he would have. Now he kicked himself for adding to it.

He didn't expect to see China at work today, and he worried that she'd never let him see her again. But that was what he deserved.

Hating to admit it, he was more like his father than he cared to be. When his mother had gotten sick, his father had withdrawn. Now he'd discovered China had a traumatic past and demons that wouldn't let go, and what did he do? He took off. He should have stuck around with Sierra.

Way to go. Now she probably thought he'd run out on her.

He'd been stunned and confused by her reaction to him seeing her legs. What the hell had gone wrong? What had happened in her past to make her react like that? He'd tried calling her several times over the weekend, but she'd left her answering-machine on and never returned his calls. Would he get a second chance to make things right?

"Code blue. Room four." One of the evening shift nurses called from a cubicle.

On automatic, Rick rushed for the crash cart. Business as usual. At least this was something he could handle.

China slid the bedpan under her patient. "Lift a little higher, Mr. Fredrickson. There we go."

She'd asked to float anywhere in the hospital rather than work in the ER. When would she learn to be careful of what she asked for? The orthopedic ward was the last place—well, second to last place—she wanted to work.

Still, it was better than facing Rick. She'd called in sick for the weekend, and Monday was her first evening back.

She pulled the bedside curtain and removed her gloves. She used the antibacterial soap from the wall dispenser and moved to the next bed for her initial assessment.

ORIF—open reduction and internal fixation—of the left femur, fractured pelvis with traction, and hairline fracture of the right ulna. Must have been one heck of a motorcycle ride. She pushed her own memories away.

She took the middle-aged man's blood pressure and scanned his temperature from the ear canal. His long silver hair was pulled back into a straggly ponytail halfway down his back. "Any numbness or tingling in your extremities?"

He stoically shook his head.

She pressed the nail beds of his left toes and right hand. There was good blood return. No evidence of edema, and she could comfortably slide her finger underneath the cast.

"I need my pain shot," he said in a gravelly voice.

She nodded, thinking he was probably used to having a cigarette dangling from his lips and might be a little edgy about the no-smoking rule. Before she could leave, the bedpan patient called out that he was ready for her.

"I'll be right with you," she said loudly toward the curtain. She turned back to her other patient. "I'll be back shortly, after I check when your last shot was." She excused herself from the traction patient and headed for the curtain.

On her way to the other bed she glanced outside to the nurses' station and saw Sierra. She was handing out fliers to all of the available employees, and left a stack on the countertop. They exchanged caring sisterly glances and wiggly finger waves across the room before Sierra left.

Later, when China was drawing up the pain shot, she curiously glimpsed one of the sheets. Sierra had written a blurb about the recent earthquake and suggested that fellow employees think of a person they had been particularly impressed with during the code orange. She gave an internet address where they could vote before the end of the week. China knew who she'd vote for. Hands down, it would be Rick.

She may have blown her chances with Rick, and he may have let her down by taking the easy way out, but there was no denying he'd been a hero the night of the earthquake.

She'd thought she'd finally worked through her past in the ladies' room on their date. How foolish of her to have thought that. Yet, in the parking lot she'd let down her guard and given herself over to Rick completely. She'd never done that before with anyone. He'd taken her to a place she'd never been before, and it had nearly scared her to death.

She'd freaked out when he'd seen her legs. She'd seen the expression on his face. No one could deny it had been a look of horror.

In all other respects he was a great guy and a dream lover, and she wished things could have worked out. Even though she'd insisted that he leave, she had really wanted him to stay, to fight for her. To fight for them.

How twisted was that? As twisted as her legs. How could the poor guy win?

As it turned out, they'd both lost.

She'd only thought she'd been ready to change, but old habits died hard. She was still punishing herself for almost finding happiness. She'd sabotaged any chance she'd had with Rick. Well, damn it, it was time to get off the guilt train.

Sick of being held hostage by her past, she made a decision to finally do something about it. It might be too late for her and Rick, but her next community-based project would be the perfect place to start being honest and exposing herself. And what a relief it would be to not have to hide any more. Now, if she could only gather enough nerve to speak in public.

A week later, at the beginning of the afternoon shift, Rick tried to avoid Sierra, but the auburn-haired older sister of his latest dating disaster wouldn't let him slip away.

She cornered him in the ER nurses' lounge, arms folded, eyes narrowed with a burning green-eyed stare. Eyes that uncomfortably reminded him of a certain woman he missed with all his soul. "You mess with my sister and you mess with me."

That got his attention.

"Listen, I've phoned her over and over again. She won't take my calls. I even went to her house and she wouldn't answer the door."

She rubbed her cheek as if thinking things through, and softened her look. "Don't give up on her."

That wasn't the tack he'd expected her to take. If

she'd cursed him and threatened to kick his ass, he'd have believed her, but this?

He scratched his neck. "For your information, she's the one who insists I'm repulsed by her legs. She wouldn't listen to anything I told her, and said I should leave. There was no changing her mind." Noting her belligerent stare, not unlike China's, he lifted his palms in surrender. "Listen, Sierra, China made things very clear. She doesn't want me around."

Sierra glanced around and lowered her voice. "You saw her. Now you know what she's been up against all these years. She needs someone to stick by her, not run away."

He worked the muscle in his jaw, choking on the words he knew he had to say. "Then she needs to quit pushing people away."

Sierra sighed. "She'll kill me for telling you, but here's the deal. Her fiancé broke off their engagement when he finally got her undressed. The bastard told her from the waist up she was perfect, but he needed the whole package. Can you imagine how that must have made her feel?"

"What? What kind of…?"

"I don't know what went down between the two of you, but she must have seen something to set her off."

Oh, hell. He'd gone clinical at the sight of her legs, and had been fascinated with what a fantastic job the orthopedic docs had done on salvaging them. How must that have looked in her eyes?

Dumbfounded, he didn't know how to reply to Sierra. Before he thought it through he said, "I tried to talk to her and she wouldn't give me the time of day."

Rick shrugged, at a loss. "Maybe the best thing I can do now is give her some space while we both work things out."

Sierra's expression hardened.

"Look, I do want your advice. It's just not a good time right now."

She unfolded her arms and walked away. He'd let China down, and had now succeeded in disappointing Sierra, too. He scrubbed his face and fought off a headache.

When he had the room to himself, he dug out the interoffice envelope marked "Confidential" from his back pocket. He recognized the personnel stamp, and cautiously opened the letter.

"We regret to inform you that you were not selected as ER Supervisor. At this time, Hospital administration has opted to continue the search with nurse practitioners rather than physicians' assistants."

He wadded it up and tossed it into the trash.

"I'm taking my break," he called out as he left the ER, heading for the stairwell. He took the stairs two at a time and hoped his anger would cool off by the time he made it to his father's office on the fourth floor.

China couldn't believe what she was hearing. After her summons, she sat across from the Mercy Hospital public relations representative in the fourth floor office, stunned.

"As I said, I'm retiring in three months, and I think you should consider applying for the job. Your track record with community events is stellar." She held up a full-page write-up, including several pictures from the local newspaper about the high school safe driving event from three weeks before. "Our hospital's name was mentioned a dozen times in this, and it places us in the lead not only as a medical facility but as a partner in the neighborhood. This kind of PR is priceless."

China gave a nervous smile and fidgeted in her chair. "But doesn't your job require public speaking?"

The silver-haired woman nodded. "I do make several appearances a month on behalf of Mercy Hospital, but most of my time is spent here at my desk, making plans."

China shuddered at the thought of public appearances. The woman must have picked up on it and backed off. She steepled her fingers and sat back in her chair, staring intently at China. During an extended silence she tapped her index fingers together, as though working things out in her mind.

China cleared her throat.

"Listen," the other woman said. "Why don't you think about it? It's an opportunity you may not want to pass up. I'm only going to retire once. I'd like to see this job go to the right person."

Nodding her head, China stood and prepared to leave. "Thank you so much for thinking about me. I promise to consider the offer." She withdrew toward the door. "Oh," she said, "so is everything a go for next month's community fundraiser for more safe teen driving programs?"

The woman glanced at the figures on the pages China had handed her when she'd first walked in.

"Yes, this looks good. And the fact that your last event came in under budget allows us to cover some of the bigger costs. I think this event will be a big neighborhood draw. Go ahead with your plans. I'm sure the budget committee will agree."

"Thanks," China chirped, feeling elated for the first time in two weeks.

She rushed out the door in time to see Rick barreling his way down the hall. He moved like a man on a mission, ready to ignite some emotional fireworks.

Feeling the wind sucked out of her when their eyes met, she stepped back against the wall. He faltered on his determined path. Knowing she owed him an explanation, an apology even, she couldn't bring herself to speak. He looked expectantly at her. Embarrassed by her lack of courage, she looked away.

He brushed past her to his father's office two doors down.

She watched him enter. If she hadn't blown it between them for good before, her silence had certainly done it now.

Dr. Morell was sitting at his desk, glasses on the end of his nose, reading a stack of papers, when Rick barged into his office. He glanced up with a glint of surprise in his eyes and moved back in his chair. In a flash he toughened his face with new resolve.

"Did you have anything to do with me not getting the job?"

Surprise crossed the older man's face.

"I've been passed over twice now." Rick leaned knuckles on the desk, and drilled his father with a vitriolic glare. "My interview went great. My job performance reviews are impeccable. Attendance: perfect.

Skills: top notch. What went wrong? And why do I think you had something to do with it?"

Dr. Morell removed his glasses and tossed them on his desk. He pinned Rick with a no-nonsense stare. "I warned you that your constant need to bend or break the rules could hold you back. Sit down," he said, in a commanding tone.

Rick straightened up, looking down at his father in defiance. "I'll stand."

After a moment's hesitation the white-haired man leaned forward, rested his elbows on the desk and cast angry eyes upward. "You've never listened to me before, so why start now? I felt my input was important to the personnel committee, and I expressed my concerns. Last time I checked, this is still a free country, isn't it? The fact that they listened shows the respect I hold from my peers."

"All it shows me is that you know how to bully and manipulate people to get what you want." Filled with restless anger, Rick paced. "It never worked with me, and it's bothered the hell out of you all my life." He stopped in his tracks to glare at his father. "If I'd done everything you wanted me to do as a kid, would things have been different?"

"Perhaps."

"You son of a bitch." He went back to leaning on the desk. "You treated me like a dog jumping through hoops. Every time I got close, you moved the hoop further away. And Mom did everything you wanted, but when she needed you the most, you abandoned her. I could never trust someone like you."

Dr. Morell rose to meet Rick's stare, raising his voice

to match his son's. "I loved your mother. I still do. And I made sure she had the finest medical care and the best bedside nursing available."

"You still don't get it, do you? She needed you to be there for her, not some nurses' aide."

Nose to nose, they glowered at each other, until Dr. Morell sat down.

"You're getting off point here," he said, lowering his voice. "We're talking about you not getting a job that you obviously thought you deserved. Being my son may have benefits in life, none of which you've ever wanted to take advantage of. But I didn't want it to look like nepotism and have the nurse practitioners who applied challenge Mercy Hospital's decision for ER supervisor."

"What right did you have to step in and quash my chances for advancement? Does everything have to be about political correctness?"

"I owe it to the hospital," he snapped back. "As the head of Internal Medicine, I must put the hospital first."

"I'm not a puppet that you can control. That's what's always bothered you about me, isn't it? You've never been able to crush my independence." Rick prepared to leave. "Well, here's a newsflash. You were so worried about the nurse practitioners challenging Mercy Hospital's choice. I'm going to be the one to do it." He jabbed at the air with his finger. "I'll take this to the hospital union if I have to. We'll see who backs down first."

Before he did anything he'd regret, he stormed out the door, slamming it.

Still in a rage, he pictured China's face. She'd turned

away from him in the hall. So that was the way it was going to be.

Her forced himself to calm down and think things through a bit more. If nothing else, China had gotten him to face up to his father.

Sierra met China on their dinner break in the cafeteria. Concern colored Sierra's eyes. She offered a single-arm hug when China sat down beside her. "How are you feeling?"

"I'm OK." After putting her food tray on the table, she hugged her sister back.

"Hey, you're wearing a skirt."

"They're culottes. It's getting warmer these days, and they're pretty comfortable to work in." China smoothed the fabric with the palms of her hands.

"Well, whatever you call them, it's great to see you in a skirt again."

Desperately wanting to move the subject away from her newest venture with change, China asked, "How's life in the ER?"

"Same old, same old." Sierra attacked her extra-large salad like a woman who hadn't eaten in days.

"Orthopedics is killing my back." China pretended to eat by moving her vegetables around her plate. "My legs throb by the end of a shift. That's why I'm wearing these extra-thick support hose."

"Why don't you come back to the ER?"

"You know I can't do that. Besides, I'm considering a new opportunity in hospital public relations. I've even signed up for a public speaking class. Can you believe it?"

Sierra looked pleased about China showing the first signs of life since she and Rick had had their blow-up.

"That's fantastic. You've got an incredible story to tell, and I think it would help your cause if you did."

China sighed, afraid to consider the unthinkable.

"Hey," Sierra said. "There's lots of scuttlebutt in the ER. Rick didn't get the supervisor job and he's furious."

"That's so unfair. If anyone deserves that job, it's Rick. I saw him storm into Dr. Morell's office this afternoon and could hear the fireworks all the way out by the elevator. I'm pretty sure he told him exactly what was on his mind."

"He's talking about going to the union or quitting altogether."

"Oh, no!" China exclaimed. "That would be a tremendous loss for Mercy Hospital."

"We all agree, but apparently Administration doesn't see it that way."

"What a waste of a good man. It'd be horrible to…" The obvious comparison of business with personal life made China falter. "To…to lose him."

Sierra lifted one brow. "I agree. That's why I'm making my newsletter poll public tomorrow. An overwhelming number of employees voted Rick Morell the employee of the year. Just about everyone had something good to say about his involvement in the code orange last month. It's time Administration, namely Dr. Morell, realized it, too."

Maybe she couldn't hope for a relationship with Rick, but at least she could help him get the job he wanted and deserved. Feeling hopeful, China had another suggestion to make. "Why don't you personally deliver the results to Dr. Morell?"

An impish grin spread across Sierra's round face.

"Great minds think alike, but I have an even better idea. I think I'll have one of Mercy Hospital's biggest financial patrons deliver it to him. Mom."

China widened her eyes and covered her mouth, and she and her sister giggled. "Perfect."

Sierra's beeper went off.

China glanced at her watch, noting her break was up and it was time to get back to the orthopedic ward.

"I'd love to be a fly on the wall in that meeting."

Two days later, Dr. Morell, after an urgent morning phone call from an important hospital patron, met Cass Seabury at the door to his office.

She waltzed into the room in a loud, multicolored caftan, practically filling out the wide dress. She gave a bland smile and offered a businesslike handshake.

He reciprocated, and accompanied her to the chair across from his desk. After she had settled in, he circled around to his own chair.

On task as a concerned medical professional, he placed his hands on the desk, one atop the other, and looked earnestly at his guest and hospital patron. "How may I help you, Ms. Seabury?"

"I have a bit of information that I thought you might be interested in." She whipped out a brightly colored piece of paper from her basket-like purse and waved it in the air. "As you may know, my daughter Sierra is the unofficial hospital newsletter editor.

"Granted, it is an underground newspaper." She smiled widely with a hint of pride. "She did the same thing in high school and college. Takes a bit after me in that regard. Rebellious." She drawled the word, with a sparkle in her bright green eyes, as though he should be excited about what she had to say. "Anyway, my point is, those in charge don't always keep their hands on the pulse of the hospital."

She passed the piece of paper across the desk for him to study. He placed his glasses on the end of his nose and pretended to be interested.

"Notice the headline."

"Rick Morell voted most valuable employee by his peers for the second year in a row."

She sat quietly and waited for him to read the rest of the story.

"Notice that there are several accounts of heroic actions that your son has taken, above and beyond the call of duty, to maintain the high quality of care expected by Mercy Hospital."

He grunted and read on. How dared she lecture him on his own son's medical merits? With great care he hid his thoughts.

"This is far from scientific data, Ms. Seabury."

"I think you're missing the point."

"The point being that my son is respected by his peers?"

She pushed the air with her finger. "Bingo."

Cass looked expectantly at him, but he refused to acknowledge she'd outsmarted him. Her bright, green-eyed stare revealed quick thoughts coursing through her mind.

"As you know, Dr. Morell, my family's trust fund has a long history with Mercy Hospital. We've provided several large donations over the years for your building projects, the most advanced medical equipment, and research."

"Yes, of course I do, Ms. Seabury." He nodded appreciatively, with a half-hearted smile and a sense of dread creeping up his spine. "And for that, we at Mercy Hospital are deeply grateful."

"Both of my daughters are employed by the hospital, and we all wholeheartedly believe in the facility's medical mission statement. 'To serve the ill and healing with the best and brightest.'"

He nodded, advancing to a pleased smile. How good he'd gotten in his role as one of the hospital administrators, at feigning interest in what others thought he needed to know. The trick was maintaining control, his only real source of power.

Using a plump hand to puff up her full head of graying red hair, she looked casually around the room. "The thing is, I'm a bit distressed by one of the current decisions made by hospital Administration." She crossed her leg and sandal-clad foot, and leaned forward. "Distressed enough to consider withdrawing this year's donation."

Dr. Morell lifted his brow with concern. "Oh? Which decision is that, Ms. Seabury? Perhaps I can put a word in to Administration on your behalf."

"Granted I'm no medical professional, but I do recognize quality when I see it. I believe it would be a grave mistake not to promote Rick Morell to the supervisory position in the ER."

Everything came clearly into focus. He furrowed his brows. "Are you attempting to blackmail me, Ms. Seabury?"

She sat primly in the chair and offered a sly smile. "I believe I am, sir."

He sighed, pursed his lips, and glanced around the office. So she'd beat him at his own game. Several strained moments of silence ensued while he thought.

Finally recognizing his own defeat for the greater good of the hospital, he looked Cass Seabury in the eyes, trying hard not to show his anger at her interference. "I'll see what I can do."

"Who can take the admission?" the charge nurse queried her staff shortly after the change of shift from day to evening.

China checked her clipboard. She had four patients assigned to her, but one, an arthroscopy patient, would be discharged tomorrow, Friday morning. "I can take another patient. What's the admitting diagnosis?"

"Broken hip. Pre-op."

No sooner had she agreed to add another patient to her assignment than the elevator doors opened and a gurney rolled out. Instead of an orderly delivering the patient from ER, Rick was at the helm. Her heart exploded into a thousand butterflies and her mouth went dry.

She hadn't seen him since he'd pushed his way into his father's office a couple of days before, and the magnitude of her body's response almost made her lose her balance. Feeling the blood drain from her face, she leaned on the counter for support, pretending to read a chart, trying to look blasé.

He rolled the gurney her way, grinning like a man with a purpose. "What room is Mr. Stewart going in?"

She couldn't make her mouth move, so she pointed to the room.

"Follow me, I'll give you report," he said.

He pushed past and she dutifully tagged along, praying she wouldn't stumble or tremble conspicuously. Her heart pounded in her chest and her breathing felt out of sync. She stopped just outside the room to recover a modicum of control.

She could do this.

She put on her nursing face and stepped inside. "Hello, Mr. Stewart."

"This is the beautiful nurse I was telling you about," Rick said with a grin to an appreciative, white-haired patient. "She'll take good care of you, I guarantee." He rolled the gurney beside the hospital bed and pumped it up to slightly above the other bed.

"China, this is Mr. Stewart. He took a fall at home this morning and broke his hip. Hip replacement surgery is scheduled for tomorrow morning. I've already called the ortho tech to come up and apply Buck's traction for tonight."

Rick walked around to the other side of the bed and rolled the draw sheet up close to the patient's body. China joined him and held the same sheet down toward the legs. Their hands touched, setting off a domino effect of goose-bumps from her arm to the base of her neck. Could he feel it, too?

"One, two, three," he counted, and on cue they both pulled the patient toward them onto the hospital bed, Rick doing the lion's share of the work.

Mr. Stewart let out a little "Ouch" but quickly settled into the bed.

"I medicated him before I brought him up. We've ordered the pre-op labs—the phlebotomist should be here soon to draw them."

Sounding so businesslike, China worried that Rick had already gotten over her and moved on. But then they looked up at the same moment and caught each other's glance. Enough sparks flew to ignite the oxygen system on the wall.

Going hot and then cold, she couldn't draw her eyes away from his piercing stare. He responded with a knowing look, mesmerizing her with heat and desire.

"Could someone cover me up? I'm getting cold," Mr. Stewart said.

China clicked back into reality.

"Oh. Of course." She rushed to pull the blanket over her patient. She raised the bedrails and fluffed his pillow. "I'll be right back for the admission interview, and I'll bring some sheepskin heel protectors, too."

"OK, Mr. Stewart, best of luck with the surgery. I'll come to see you tomorrow, like I promised."

"I'm going to hold you to it, young man."

"Sure thing."

Rick rolled the empty gurney toward the door. China held back, keeping a safe distance, waiting for him to leave, grateful that she had tomorrow off and wouldn't have to see him again.

Once she stepped outside the door, she felt his firm grasp on her wrist leading her toward the supply room. Electricity coursed up her arm to her shoulders and down her spine from his touch.

He pulled her inside and closed the door. "Why haven't you answered any of my calls?"

"Uh…"

She'd hardly had a chance to catch her breath when his mouth covered hers. She melted into his arms and marveled at the velvet warmth of his kiss. Immediate memories of his muscular, naked body covering hers sent shivers through her core. The woman on fire, the part of her who'd been missing since their goodbye, came back to life.

She could and would survive without him, but he made her life sweeter. She leaned against the counter and kissed him back while vaguely realizing she was at work and making out in the supply room. She didn't care.

He abruptly broke off the kiss long before she was ready. His penetrating chocolate-colored eyes looked deep into her soul. She shook her head to help concentrate on his words.

"For the record," he said, tersely, "my reaction to your legs was shock and pain for you, because I care about you. How they look makes no difference to me. My feelings haven't changed, but until you believe that there is no hope for us."

He shoved his hands into his pockets and prepared to leave. "When you're ready to talk, you know where to find me," he said, in a sonorous voice. He opened the door. "By the way," he said, over his shoulder, "nice skirt."

Breathless and shaken all the way down to her toes, she worked to recover and said, "They're culottes."

CHAPTER TEN

THE next evening, China's day off, she joined Sierra for dinner at her house. Mother Cass sat with a cat-like grin, bouncing a protesting Timmy on her knee.

"I'm too old for this, Grammy."

She pinched his cheek. "You're never too old for your Grandma's lap."

He wriggled off and escaped her playful, tickly grasp and shot out of the room.

Sierra served after-dinner tea, and sat with China on the kitchen bench on the other side of the table. "Come on. Spill. What happened?"

China pretended to be only mildly interested in her mother's story.

"He's a tough one, that Lawrence Morell, but not as tough as this old broad." Cass laughed and slapped her knee.

Sierra rolled her eyes and watched China for a reaction.

China kept a poker face, refusing to divulge her eager and expectant feelings.

"OK. As you know, money talks. When he didn't

budge about Rick, after I showed the newsletter and poll results, I cut to the chase and hit him where it hurts. Mercy Hospital's pocket book. They've been contacting me lately regarding a new building project they want to undertake in the gastroenterology wing. Remember last year our family trust donated all of the upgraded endoscopes?"

China and Sierra both nodded.

"Well, now they need a new room with special radiation-resistant walls and all. We're talking a hundred thou, easy, and they'd like me to donate a portion of it. You should have seen him squirm when I firmly suggested his son was the best man for the ER job, and then in my next breath I brought up the trust fund."

She laughed again, a loud cackle that brought Timmy back into the kitchen.

"What's so funny, Grammy?"

"Life is, hon. It's a real hoot. Enjoy every minute of it."

Timmy twisted up his face and glanced suspiciously at his mom. "OK," he said, rushing back out of the room.

As though he'd had a second thought, he stuck his head back inside the kitchen. "Aunt China?"

"Yes?"

"When can I play checkers with Rick again?"

China blushed. "Oh, well…"

"I want to kick his butt again."

"Watch your language, squirt," Sierra said.

Timmy screwed up his face and glanced at the ceiling.

"Gee, I don't know, Timmy." China hemmed and hawed until her nephew lost interest and left the room.

"Soon, if I have anything to do with it," Sierra said under her breath.

China kicked her under the table.

"Ouch!"

"Now, girls," Cass chided. "Let me finish my story."

Both dying to know yet apprehensive to hear the end, China grew quiet.

"So I got all serious and looked Lawrence Morell square in the eyes and said, 'I'm concerned about the decision you've made about the ER supervisor job.' Then I hit him with the old one-two. 'I'm considering withholding my annual donation,' I said.

"His eyes got big as saucers, but he caught himself real quick-like and put on his administrative face."

Sierra's hand flew to her mouth to squelch a giggle.

"Get this. He says, 'Are you blackmailing me, Ms. Seabury?' And I say…" Cass put on an air of grandeur "'…I believe I am, Dr. Morell.'" She hit the table with her palm, causing the teacups to rattle.

China jumped and refrained from making a fist and tugging the air with a little victory salute.

"Way to go, Ma." Sierra reached across the table and patted her mother on the back.

"Money talks, girls, money talks. When you both turn thirty, you'll get your trust-fund money and you'll know how it feels to be independently wealthy." Looking pleased, she slid back in her chair and nibbled on a cookie.

"I got mine last year, remember, Ma?"

Cass looked shocked, as though she couldn't fathom her eldest daughter already having reached the age of thirty.

"Who knows if social security will always be around? I'm using it for our retirement fund and Timmy's college education," Sierra said. "In case he wants to go to medical school." She grinned. "And a super-nice vacation or two."

"You know how I intend to use most of mine," China mumbled, before sipping her tea. "That is, after I buy my first house."

"Right. National teenage driver education. Where the hell did I go wrong?" Cass glanced toward the ceiling as though she expected an answer from there. "There isn't an ounce of self-indulgence between the two of you."

"Oh, really?" Sierra said, with a challenge. "Watch this," she said as she took a second cookie and devoured it.

Rick sat across from D'Wayne in the fast-food restaurant booth.

"Do you want your fries?" D'Wayne asked.

"Nah. I'm not hungry."

"Dude, you still gamin' on China?" He eagerly stuffed a trio of fries in his mouth.

"That's none of your business."

"You're acting like my old lady."

"Your mother," Rick corrected.

"Yeah, yeah, whatever. She always wants to run my business, but I can't know anything about hers."

"She doesn't want to worry you. That's all."

"And she's always baggin' on me, too. Do this. Don't do that. Listen to me. I know what's best. Dang." He gave an exasperated eye roll and glance. "Now every time I ask to use the car, she waves that agreement I signed in my face."

"It's her way of showing she loves you."

"She sure has a whack way of showing it."

"It's her job to bug you."

"I know. But cut me some slack. I'm sixteen."

Rick thought back to the defiant teenager he'd once been, always in his father's face about things, bound and determined to do the opposite of whatever his father said.

He thought about how he had always felt there were strings attached to his dad's affection, and how he refused to play that game.

Hard-headed pride was all it was. The same kind of reaction he saw in D'Wayne resisting his mother and her "conditions" for driving.

Something clicked in his brain.

The oddest thing occurred to him. He'd been guilty of doing the exact same thing he'd accused his father of doing—withholding his love for his dad until he acted the way Rick expected him to. He'd been self-righteously expecting unconditional love, but had only offered conditional love himself.

Hell, he'd been no different than his old man all along.

"Did you hear anything I just said?" D'Wayne tugged Rick's sleeve, looking impatient.

"What? Uh. No. What'd you say?"

D'Wayne pushed his fast-food tray away. "Never mind, man. I already ate the rest of your burger."

Rick glanced at his empty tray unfazed, and stood up.

"Where're you goin'?" D'Wayne asked, gathering up their debris.

"I gotta see a man about an apology."

Rick hadn't paid a visit to his childhood home since Christmas, six months ago, and then, even though surrounded by family and friends, it had been strained and tiresome. He stood on the doorstep with rattled nerves. It was nine o'clock in the evening, but he didn't care. When you knew something was right, you didn't waste time. He'd put this overdue encounter off long enough, and it was finally time to face his past, namely his dad.

Dr. Morell opened the door in a tattered gold golf sweater and baggy brown slacks. Surprise and confusion battled it out for dominant expression, followed by the look that hit home and put Rick to shame: suspicion. He could only imagine what might be running through his father's head with him showing up out of nowhere after their last antagonistic meeting.

"Rick?" Immediately on the defensive, his father's expression hardened with a glare. "I'm in no mood for another argument."

"I'm not here to argue, Dad." Rick felt calmness settle inside his racing heart. Finally, he resolved to make the right decision where his father was concerned.

"I don't appreciate you sending your big guns to blackmail me either."

"What are you talking about?"

"Don't tell me you didn't put Cass Seabury up to paying me a visit."

"I don't have a clue what you're talking about."

"Hmm. It must have been those daughters of hers."

His father hesitated, grasped the doorknob, and jiggled the change in his trousers, not budging.

Rick shifted from one foot to the other. He cleared his throat, smiled at his father, and meant it. "I thought I'd stop by before I went in to work. I traded my shift with one of the night PA's." He scrubbed his jaw and took a deep breath.

Oh, what the hell.

"Look, I'm sorry, Dad."

Bewilderment shifted across his father's face. He glanced at his watch. "Well, it's not too late, I suppose," he said, and opened the door a bit wider.

"No," Rick said, putting his hand on his father's shoulder as he edged into his childhood home. "I'm afraid it's long overdue, and I really mean it. I came here to say I'm sorry. I hope it's not too late to say it, but I'm sorry about everything." He looked sincerely into his father's eyes. "And I want you to know that, no matter what, I love you."

Dr. Morell blocked the entry and offered a cautious glance, one that suggested that Rick might have flipped his lid. "Are you in one of those twelve-step programs or something?"

Rick laughed. "No. I mean it. I love you, Dad."

"What's the catch?"

"Nothing," Rick said, and raised his hand in surrender. "*Nada.* Zippo. It's called unconditional love, and I figured it was about time I learned how to give it."

Rick thought he saw a flicker of recognition in his father's eyes. It didn't matter if the look was for the wrong reason or not. He didn't care if his father's expression was a victorious grin or a genuinely pleased smile. Nothing mattered but what was written on his heart: sincerity.

His father stepped aside to allow Rick to enter.

After years at war with his dad, he sensed a glimmer of hope as he stepped inside. And for the first time in his adult life, Rick felt as if he was finally his own man.

China rubbed bleary eyes. She'd practiced her first speech for class a dozen times, tweaked it until it sounded exactly the way she wanted, and practiced it again and again. Her stomach got queasy each time she thought about tomorrow's assignment. It was necessary, though. She'd made the decision to take the lead in her life, instead of letting her past control her.

After one last speech rehearsal, she gathered up her paperwork for the community fair the next weekend. She studied the list of participants, made check marks by those who'd already committed themselves, and highlighted the people she still needed to contact.

At close to one a.m. she crawled into bed, satisfied that in every other aspect of her life, except where Rick was concerned, things were going well.

Making herself a promise that she would deal with Rick the following week, after the community awareness fundraiser for safe teenage driving, she turned off the light. The thought of facing him sent a hailstorm of fear through her heart, but she owed herself one last chance at happiness.

Something woke her at a quarter to four. Disoriented, China sat up and tried to gather her wits. Was the alarm going off? Was it already time to get up? She followed the piercing sound to the phone and picked up the receiver.

"Hello?"

"It's Sierra. Come quick. Mom's on her way in to the ER."

The next moments blurred by. China blew through her house. She threw on her clothes, splashed water in her face and brushed her teeth. In the car, driving faster than she'd ever allow herself normally, she shot onto the freeway.

Shaking and fumbling with the combination buttons on the entry pad to the ER door, she dropped her purse and tried again. Her mind was in a shambles, her hands jittered, and she couldn't remember the code to get in. The doors swung open. Someone from inside must have seen her and pushed the buzzer to allow her to enter.

The night charge nurse, with an empathetic glance, pointed to the cubicle swarming with paramedics, doctors, nurses, her sister, and Rick.

Rick? He must be doing a double shift. A bolt of hope for her mother coursed through her.

Sierra rushed to her side, grabbed China's arm and held tight. Intense eyes glowed out from her white face. "She woke up with severe jaw pain and at first thought she was having indigestion, but it got worse. She called me and I called 911. I told her to take an aspirin, breathe deeply and cough hard and often until the paramedics arrived."

China understood that heart attacks manifested themselves differently in women than men. Her mother's jaw pain may have been more indicative of an MI than the usual chest pain and extreme pressure for a man. Taking deep breaths would have forced oxygen through her lungs and deep coughing would have massaged her heart. Doing both together might even have generated enough energy to break the life-threatening heart rhythm. Sierra had thought of everything and the suggestions may have bought precious time and saved her mother's life.

They hugged each other in relief. "You did good, sis."

"Her heart rhythm is all over the place. Looks like an elevated ST segment on the EKG. Rick gave her nitroglycerin and morphine. The labs have been drawn and oxygen is in place. All we can do is wait and hope for the best."

"She's in good hands now," China said.

Sierra nodded, and together they watched the emergency technicians leave and the on-call doctor and Rick take over. One nurse fussed with the IV, as though it had stopped running.

Rick applied a tourniquet to Cass's other arm and expertly slid in a new intravenous line in no time at all, switching the saline bag from the infiltrated IV to the new one.

The heart monitor alarm started blaring. China watched as Rick's head shot up. The other doctor said something to him and he dashed for the crash cart. She fought the impulse as a nurse to run into the room, but knew her emotions about her own mother being the patient would make her useless.

Sierra squeezed her hands and they stood helpless

and frozen in place as Rick announced, "Code blue. We've got a code."

Though out of fashion, the doctor gave a precordial thump to Cass's sternum to help jump-start her heart before Rick returned with the cart.

Rick helped the nurse set up the ambubag for ventilation, and once in place and aerating her mother he began external compressions. A second nurse applied the pre-jelled defibrillator pads and turned on the machine. An eerie mechanical voice announced the dangerous rhythm. "Ventricular tachycardia. Deliver shock."

The doctor called, "All clear." Everyone stepped away from the bed. The machine automatically delivered the shock via the pads. After the shock was delivered, Rick immediately continued compressions as the nurse used the ambubag to breathe for her mother.

The on-call anesthesiologist and pharmacist both arrived, looking rumpled, with their emergency equipment, as if they'd been awakened from the sleeping rooms. One doctor stepped toward Cass's head and the other stood by the IV.

The pharmacist injected a bolus of what China assumed was epinephrine into the IV as CPR continued. The anesthesiologist tilted Cass's head back and attempted to slide an airway into her throat. The first try wasn't successful. He repositioned her head, and re-applied the bellows over her mouth and nose to artificially breathe for her while CPR continued.

"Deliver shock," the machine instructed again.

"All clear."

Rick stopped his compressions and stepped away. So

did the anesthesiologist. Rick briefly glanced at Sierra and China, his face contorted with concern.

China held her breath.

After the electrical jolt and a straight-line pause, a slow sinus rhythm blipped across the monitor screen.

The anesthesiologist tried again to intubate Cass, but her hand shot up and grabbed his wrist, startling him.

China smiled as her heart quivered with hope. She squinted to watch the monitor above the bed.

Finally, the alarm stopped.

She glanced at her sister and burst into tears. They clung to each other like they might disappear if they didn't hold each other tight. She thanked the heavens for delivering their mother into the best hands possible when having a heart attack and, more importantly, for their mother having the sheer will to survive. The ever-rebellious Cass would have nothing to do with death, not tonight anyway.

The specialists cleared out of the patient cubicle. Only the doctor, one nurse, and Rick remained.

China saw Rick linger, pat her mother's hand reassuringly, smile and say something, when he thought no one was looking.

She'd heard him say it before to other patients after codes, and if she remembered it correctly, it went something like, "Welcome back, Ms. Seabury. It's going to be a great day."

Her heart lurched when her mother reached up and patted his arm. She ran toward her mother, Sierra following quickly behind.

The other doctor scribbled orders on a green admission sheet. He stuck his head out the door and called to the charge nurse. "We're sending Ms. Seabury to the cath lab stat."

"If you're short on nursing staff, Sierra and I can help transport our mom."

"Since she got to the ER in less than four hours, and she's well under seventy-five, I could go with timely thrombolytic therapy," the doctor said to them. "But I think cardiac catheterization is the right thing to do this morning. We'll see where we need to go from there. Oh, and her blood pressure is low, so I'm adding a dopamine IV piggyback. And if you ladies want to help transport her to the cath lab, that's fine with me." He placed his pen behind his ear. "I don't have too many nurses to spare this morning."

"I'll go, too," Rick said in a guarded tone. He glanced at China and quickly away, all business.

China held her mother's limp hand and cast her a worn-out, reassuring glance.

"I'm not ready to say 'when' yet," Cass said in a raspy voice. "So let's do this thing and fix me up for another twenty or so years."

The doctor squeezed out a smile, retrieved his pen, and finished his notes. Rick placed the portable heart monitor on the foot of the gurney before he placed the oxygen tank by Cass's side. It hissed through the mask over Cass's face.

"I'll steer the infusion monitor," Sierra said, rolling the IV to the head of the bed.

China kicked the bed lock free and joined her sister at the front of the gurney. Rick pointed for them to go to the rear of the bed and guide it, while he pushed.

Together, the three of them headed out of the ER at six a.m., and toward the hospital employee elevators for the second floor cardiac catheter lab.

China concentrated on her mother, making sure the oxygen mask was properly in place and that the heart monitor remained intact with a normal sinus rhythm.

"Oh, quit fussing with me, China baby. They gave me something that's making me feel pretty damn good right now."

"Mom, we almost lost you tonight. I'll fuss all I want."

She helped navigate through the quiet hospital corridors to their destination, pretending to be incensed but secretly thrilled her mother was already bouncing back to her previous brazen self.

"What are you doing, working tonight, Rick?" Sierra broke the silence.

"I switched with Gavin so I can catch a plane to Seattle this afternoon. I'm interviewing for a position at the veterans' hospital there."

China's stomach dropped to her knees, and she almost tripped on the bed. What about, "When you're ready to talk, you know where to find me"? Hadn't he meant it? Had she waited too long? How foolish of her to think after the community fair would be soon enough to tell him how she felt. Her mind raced furiously with questions and fears about losing Rick, but almost losing her mother was foremost in her mind, and she brushed them away.

"But what about fighting the system and going to the union?" Sierra said, guiding the gurney a bit harder and faster.

"I've finally made peace with my father, something I came here to do two years ago. He still hasn't come around, but I'm OK with that. I don't expect him to any more." He cast a sideways glance at China. "Maybe it's time to move on."

A dagger in her chest couldn't have hurt more than the pain she felt at his words. Rather than let on, she pretended to be preoccupied with pushing the elevator button.

The rest of the transport was a blur. All that was real and exciting and treasured in her life had crumbled in one night. She studied her mother, the bold, grab-life-by-the-tail woman, who now looked alarmingly frail. She thought about Rick, ready to cut his losses and run. What was left for her? Endless fundraising?

They arrived in the cardiac cath lab and Rick gave his report to the on-call doctor and nurses. No sooner had he finished than his beeper went off.

He nodded at Sierra, then toward China.

A look that she could only describe as uncertain clouded his gaze when he lingered and searched her eyes for the beat of one breath.

"I've got to go," he said.

She couldn't find her voice to respond, so she stood mute and watched him leave until her eyes fluttered closed.

Once their mother had been rolled into the procedure room, Sierra impaled her with a fierce challenging stare. "Do you love him?"

Tears welled and China swallowed hard, fighting the urge to cry. "No. Yes." Her hands fisted. "I don't know."

"Are you going to let the catch of the century walk out like that? What the hell's the matter with you?"

"I don't know."

Fear for her mother, pain for Rick, every thought and feeling she'd suppressed over the course of the last few hours rushed out at once. She convulsed into tears.

Sierra wrapped her in her arms then rocked her. "Oh, kid. This all sucks so bad."

China collected what control she had left and wiped her eyes, trying desperately to recover. At least their mother had survived, and she had her community project to keep her distracted. And heaven only knew how much more work she had to do before all would be ready by that weekend. Weary and drained, she leaned against her sister for support.

She refused to succumb to pessimism. Feeling life spinning out of control, she refused to give in, and steeled herself for the days ahead—her mother's recovery, Rick's departure and the possibility of never seeing him again, and the biggest community event of her life.

Now the only question was whether she was strong enough to make it through it all alone. And more importantly, when the time came to finally set the public record straight, would she be ready?

CHAPTER ELEVEN

CHINA hardly slept for the next few days. What with her mother's recovery, the demands of work, and Saturday's community event, she was too nervous. She'd lain awake at night and stared at the ceiling, going through every aspect of her plans. Everything was set and the weekend loomed ahead. There was no turning back.

She practiced her welcome speech one last time before rolling out of bed to prepare for work. She'd switched with one of the day shift nurses in the ER to allow for Friday night off. There would be too many last-minute details she'd need to attend to early the next morning to work the evening shift the night before.

An hour later, she parked in the usual place in the parking lot and strolled toward the hospital. Up ahead, she thought she saw Rick's distinctive frame—tall, broad shoulders, long legs, and narrow hips but he was in street clothes instead of scrubs. He'd been gone for several days. Her heart hopped and she inhaled a quick breath. What would she say if she ran into him face to face?

Fearing that, and knowing she could never stand another farewell glance like he'd given her in the cath lab earlier in the week, she steered away and entered the side door to the first hospital floor. She stuck her head inside the double doors and peered one way and then another. The coast was clear, so she made her move and dashed toward the ER entrance.

Inside the ward, Rick stood talking to the charge nurse. They laughed and hugged awkwardly. He bade her goodbye and turned to leave. Emotional coward that she was, China ducked for cover where she could watch him unobserved. Hands now in his pockets, he came to a stop and lingered for a second with a nonchalant glance around the room.

She couldn't allow herself to hide. Hadn't she turned to a new page in her life? She took a deep breath and stepped into his path. His eyes widened with surprise.

"If you've got a minute, I'd like to talk."

"Gosh, China." He ran his hand through his hair. "I've got a meeting I'm already late for."

"I need to tell you how sorry I am for the way I acted. I want to apologize for the things I said about your relationship with your father. It was none of my business."

"Can we talk about this some other time?"

Realizing she'd lost him, her heart ached. He must have read her expression.

"Listen, don't worry about it. You did me a favor. I've got to go."

Yeah, she'd done him a favor all right. Next time, before he gets involved with anyone, he'll check out the merchandise before it's too late.

If she'd held out any hope of working things through between them, they dissolved before her eyes when he walked out the door. At least she'd made amends.

"You'll live. You can do this. It's for the best," she muttered, as she put her purse in her locker, biting back tears, and prepared for the nurses' report.

Sierra arrived in the medicine room fifteen minutes before the change from day to evening shift, breathless and excited. "I just heard they've hired someone for ER supervisor."

"Who is it?" China said, more hopeful than she cared to admit, preparing to count the narcotics with her sister.

"It's all hush-hush, but they're going to announce it on Monday."

China counted and called out numbers. Sierra carefully recorded them on the goldenrod class II drug sheet. They countersigned and took a quick break together in the nurses' lounge before China's shift ended and Sierra's began.

"I may have an announcement of my own by Monday."

Sierra's eyes widened. "What? Tell me?"

"Stay tuned, big sister."

Sierra shook her head. "You're a pain, you know that? Speaking of pain, here's Mom's grocery list. She's playing us like the lottery since she got discharged."

China took it and rolled her eyes. "Half of this stuff isn't even on her cardiac diet."

"Do you think it matters to her?"

They studied each other, both knowing that Cass would never be one to bend to conventional wisdom about anything.

"Mom and Timmy and I will drop by the park tomorrow around eleven, OK?"

China nodded, and her mouth went dry. Eleven was when she intended to give the welcome speech at the community fundraiser. A flutter of nerves made the fine hair on her neck stand on end. How would she manage to not fall apart?

The late fall weather, in typical Indian summer fashion, had taken a decidedly warm turn by Saturday morning. China pulled on a new pair of khaki shorts, the first phase of her fresh start. She hadn't shown her legs in public since her senior year in high school, ten years previously.

She stood before her mirror and examined her thin thighs and misshapen calves, covered in gashes and scars. Were they as horrible as she'd thought all these years? Bottom line—her legs were functional, and she was grateful, but still the thought of displaying them in public made her tremble.

She buttoned her short-sleeved white blouse, threw on some sandals and swept up her hair into a long ponytail. She collected her clipboard with the massive amount of papers she needed, and by seven a.m. was heading out the door for the neighborhood park.

Brilliant sunlight sparkled through the trees. Fresh air massaged her bare arms and legs. She felt invigorated with a combination of excitement and apprehension.

"Put all the face-painting supplies over here," China directed a few of the local volunteers.

A burly fireman tapped her on the shoulder. "Ms. Seabury?"

"Captain Glendower, what can I do for you?"

"We've got two fire trucks set up next to the police cruisers, and we'll have the firemen's hose race right after you give the opening address."

"That will be great." She shook his hand and glanced around the park. There must have been close to a hundred people milling around, setting up booths and equipment.

"China?" A lady approached. "Where are the tickets for the booths?"

She dug into her huge shoulder-bag, found a roll of red tickets and handed them to the volunteer.

"The pizzas are starting to arrive now. We've got the warmer ovens and heating lights in place. Oh, and the chilidog people are all set up. And ice cream will be sold over there." The woman pointed in three different directions.

The local high school band climbed out of a huge orange bus in the adjacent parking lot and unloaded their instruments, making a big racket.

The race-car simulation booth would definitely be a big draw for them. She'd schooled the facilitator to make sure he constantly reinforced her mantra, "Don't try this at home."

She'd assigned herself to the face-painting booth, and another booth down the way would show the high school video from the teen driving assembly. She'd never waste an opportunity to pound her message home: teenage driving wasn't a right. It was both a privilege and a responsibility.

She forced a deep breath and took a swig from a bottle of water. She'd do everything in her power to make the day a success.

A warm breeze brought the distinctive smell of a barbeque from across the park, and though her stomach was wound tighter than a spool of thread, her mouth watered at the aroma.

A familiar figure caught her off guard. Dr. Morell approached, looking more relaxed than she'd seen him in weeks. He was probably celebrating the departure of the constant thorn in his side, his son Rick. A bitter taste worked up the back of her throat, but she hid her dislike of the man.

"China." He extended his hand, and looked genuinely pleased to see her.

"Dr. Morell. I'm surprised to find you here today." She fought off a cold, reserved response to him. "Did you pick the short straw?"

His gray eyes glimmered in the sun when he smiled, his tan skin in stark contrast to his silver-white hair.

"Actually, I volunteered to do a couple of hours in the dunking booth."

She stopped herself from snickering, and thought about how long the line would be to throw the baseball at the lever that would drop him into the water tank once word got out.

"You're kidding, right?"

"No. Life's too short not to enjoy every minute, China." He winked and strolled off, leaving her flummoxed.

What had that been all about?

Sierra and Timmy came running her way, waving.

She smiled and returned the greeting.

Her nephew threw his arms around her waist before stepping back with huge eyes. "Wow, Aunt China, your scars are awesome. Did you get attacked by a lion or something?"

"Sort of. More like a big metal elephant."

"Wow."

Cass strolled up to the group, using a new and flashy black cane for support since the angioplasty through her femoral artery. She gave China the once-over. Her face softened at the sight of her legs, and she broke into a grin. "That's my girl."

They hugged and China kissed her mother's cheek, savoring her presence after remembering the close call in the ER the week before.

"I want to see the fire truck. Come on, Grammy and Mom."

Timmy dragged off the best women in China's life before they could make plans to meet for lunch. She figured she'd be too busy to socialize with anyone for the rest of the afternoon anyway. From the corner of her vision she saw the fire chief approach with a bullhorn in his grasp.

"Show time, Ms. Seabury. Let's get this party rolling."

She cleared her throat and headed for the makeshift stage in the center of the park, her heart doing a jitterbug in her chest.

"Attention, attention," the fire chief blared through the voice amplifier.

She did a quick mental rundown of what she needed to do. First she'd offer an innocent greeting, encourage everyone to have fun, and later, when the crowd had enjoyed themselves for a while, she'd hit them with reality and ask them to open their pocketbooks for her cause.

And though her public speaking coach had recently helped her get past her stuttering, her confidence wavered when she climbed up the steps to the stage. She recalled her coach's words. "Remember the girl who took all-county on the debate team ten years ago. Don't forget, you have the ability. Remember who you are." She'd reminded China with the same words at every meeting. At first, China had resented having her past dragged up meeting after meeting. Now she was grateful.

Yeah, it was definitely time to embrace the person she'd once been and, more importantly, accept who she had become.

She scanned the gathering crowd, recognizing many coworkers, friends and teenagers from the local schools. She waved and smiled until she thought her cheeks would turn to stone and her arm would fall off. She even thought she saw D'Wayne, wearing a bright orange bandana over his dreadlocks somewhere towards the back of the park. But maybe she was imagining things.

"Welcome, everyone." She smiled and waved more while the audience applauded. Her lower lip quivered, but she stretched her grin wider to cover it up. "Isn't it beautiful out today?" She glanced at her notes and hoped some saliva would soon form. "I want to thank our chamber of commerce for allowing us to use this fantastic park, and everyone else who has donated items or pitched in to help bring this event together. And most of all I want to thank Mercy Hospital for seeing a need to educate teenagers about their responsibility as new drivers, and pursuing it by raising public awareness.

We've got lots of fun planned today, so eat, keep hydrated, and enjoy yourselves. But first the Valley View High School swing band is going to start things off."

She clapped along with the crowd as the youthful conductor took the stage and a lively rendition of one of the Beatles' early songs started up in a marching band arrangement. At the very first opportunity she snuck off the stage to head for a bathroom where she could recover from her nerves before she started painting faces.

So far, so good, she reassured herself as she walked.

Determined to survive the day, she instinctively knew the rest of her life depended on it.

"Were you in an accident or something?" asked what seemed like the millionth kid of the afternoon.

"Yes, a long time ago. I'm lucky to be alive," she said when she'd finished painting the child's cheeks. On a whim she painted the tip of the girl's upturned nose kitten pink, then drew whiskers on her cheeks. "So when you grow up, you must promise to be a safe driver, OK?"

"OK."

A tall shadow surprised her when her next customer stepped up. "D'Wayne?"

"Yeah."

"What are you doing here?"

"I want my face painted. Dang, what happened to your legs?"

"Long story."

He glanced at them again, and must have figured that

was all he needed to know. "You got any fluorescent paint?"

"Sure."

"I want you to paint 'Will you go out with me?' on my head," he said, and removed his bandana. "Right here." He pointed to his forehead. "Then, tonight at the movies, I'll take this off, and Desiree will see it in the dark. Cool, huh?"

"Sit down, D'Wayne. I'm confused. Aren't you already going to be on a date?"

He nodded.

"So why ask her to go out with you tonight?"

"Going out is different than going on a date."

She stirred the brush in fluorescent yellow. "Now I'm really puzzled." She started to paint.

"Asking her to go out makes her my girlfriend."

"Whatever." China shook her head, mystified by the current teenage terminology for going steady and dating. She soon finished her task of painting the message on his forehead. "Here," she said, handing him a mirror. "Make sure to let it dry before you put your bandana back on."

He smiled, "Dude. That's off the heezy."

"I'm glad you like it, but I'm a dudette." She glanced at her watch, realizing it was time for her speech. Her previously efficient lungs lurched to a halt. "Listen, I've got to go." She sounded breathless. "Be sure to let me know how your proposal turns out."

She picked up her notes with trembling hands and stuffed them back into her purse, deciding to speak from her heart instead.

"Are you OK?" he asked.

"I'll be fine," she said, taking one last gulp of water and striding with determination toward the stage.

On her way, she heard a huge splash and loud cheers coming from the dunking cage where Dr. Morell held court, and smiled. Sweet justice.

Fire Captain Glendower, still soaking wet from the hose relays, used the bullhorn to quieten down the crowd.

A large banner of a crashed and mangled car got unfurled behind the stage, with the before and after accident photos of Brianna Cummings hanging next to it. One of the firemen ran the siren for a few seconds.

Having the audience's full attention, China stepped to the microphone, aware that everyone who hadn't noticed her legs before did so now.

"Before I invite Mayor Dixon to speak, I'd like to tell you a story about a beautiful summer day ten years ago." She cleared her throat and began her story, hoping she'd be able to stay composed. "My best friend and I were heading to the beach. We had the car radio blasting and we swayed to our favorite song." She snapped her fingers and swung her hips back and forth. "We were having a ball, and I was driving. I glanced at Amy and joked, 'Look! No hands.'" She grew silent and stared at the audience for a couple of seconds. "And that's the last thing I remember."

She paused to allow her tale to sink in and also to gather her thoughts. She bit her lip and prayed she'd be able to finish her story. "Two days later, I woke up in the hospital in traction with pins, metal and wires sticking out of one leg and the other in a full-length cast. I had already had one surgical procedure and was told

I would have several others before I could use my legs again." She glanced at her legs. "They were doubtful that I would ever walk normally again. I know, they don't look so hot, do they?" She walked back and forth across the stage so everyone could see. "But they work. And I was the lucky one." She choked back the urge to cry, swallowed hard and blinked.

She took a deep and ragged breath.

"You see, Amy died that day, and it was…" Her eyes welled up and she swallowed hard. She wiped them with a trembling hand. "It was, uh, my fault."

Not a sound could be heard from the audience.

Air caught in her lungs. Her lower lip quivered. "We all make mistakes. Some you can fix, but some you can never take back." She sniffed, fought back more tears, and gathered her composure. "My hope and dream is that none of you teenagers ever have to go through what I've had to experience." Her voice cracked. She pounded a fist into her other hand, knowing this was her one shot to drive the point home. Fired up, she went for it. "That's why we're all hitting you so hard about the privilege of driving. Heck, we live in a world of iPods, cellphones, Mac attacks, and far too many other distractions. But even one second of inattention behind the wheel can be fatal.

"When you take someone's life away, a part of you dies with them. It takes time to heal the body, and longer to heal the soul."

Her gaze swept across the gathered crowd. She saw Rick off to the right and felt suddenly off balance. Her heart jumped in her chest, and she decided to add something meant only for him. "And until the soul is healed, you just keep on hurting yourself and the ones you love. Believe me. I know. I've done it all."

She looked at Rick. "And when the people who love you can look past your scars and still care, you doubt them. Because you can't believe you deserve such joy when your best friend is dead, and it was your fault."

She took a deep breath to keep from breaking down, deciding to wrap things up. "So when you're driving, don't drink, disconnect, or tune out. Be sure to buckle up. Stay focused. And if you haven't done so already, go to the Valley View High School booth and watch the video we made last month. Teenage accidents happen every fifteen minutes, and people of all ages are dying." Being true to her crusade, she wasn't too proud to beg. "Please, do your part, donate money for the cause, and drive carefully."

After a brief pause, and long and heart-warming applause, she had the presence of mind to introduce the mayor before she left the stage.

No sooner had her feet hit the grass then a field reporter from the local news station approached with both a cameraman and soundman in tow.

She saw Rick nearby and caught his attention, knowing she might never have another chance to talk to him. Buoyed by her recent confession, she called out, "I'm working the face-painting booth. Please, come and see me."

"Ms. Seabury, we've just recorded your speech. How much money do you hope to raise for your cause?"

Tearing her gaze from Rick, she focused back on the reporter.

"Mercy Hospital is hoping to raise $50,000 today. But the amount of lives it could save with driver awareness training is priceless."

"If a parent wanted to purchase one of the videos for their child, how would they go about it?"

"Go to the Mercy Hospital website and click on the teenage driving icon."

"OK. Easy enough. We at MXW network hope today's event is a great success."

"Thank you. If your television station is interested, we have a matching fund program for employee donations. We'd love to have you on board."

Looking a bit flustered, he nodded and said, "You heard the lady. Signing out from Central City Park, Jess Atkins, for MXW news."

China didn't know if one minute or fifty had passed. All she knew was the incredible rush of relief that washed over her. She'd finally confessed her sins in public. She felt as though a thousand pounds of brick had been lifted from her chest. She could breathe deeper now, stand taller, and even see clearer. Almost euphoric, she strode back to her face-painting booth, ready to volunteer more time.

While organizing her paint and brushes, another large shadow loomed over her. But this time the hairs on her arms and the back of her neck stood on end. Both afraid and eager to turn around, she took a deep breath and slowly rotated in the chair, hoping she would see the man she loved.

Rick stood before her in all his glory, with a blinding sunburst behind him. She couldn't make out his features, but she'd recognize the shape of him and his full head of coffee-and-cream-colored hair anywhere. She stared until it hurt, until her eyes adjusted and she could finally see his face.

He looked at her like a man who'd been on another planet, one without women, for several years, first sweeping his gaze from her head then all the way down to her sandals.

With an eruption of nerves, she forced small talk. "How was Seattle?"

"I didn't like the scenery," Rick said.

He went back to staring at her legs and clicked his tongue. "Nice." He plopped five red tickets on her counter. "I want my face painted."

"Not so fast. How did your interview go?"

"Great. They loved me." He pointed to the tickets. "I want my face painted," he said again.

Completely undone by his presence and his less than forthcoming remarks about an interview that would change his life and the course of their relationship, she objected. "I can't paint your face."

"Sure you can. I paid my money." He waved the tickets in the air.

She held her hands before him to show him how much they trembled. "I can't even pick up a brush right now, let alone paint."

Looking pleased at the affect he had on her, he crossed his arms, stroked his chin, and said, "Here's an idea. I'll paint your face first. Then you can paint mine."

She tried to give him an "as if" glance, but, feeling completely flustered, she wasn't sure if the look was sassy or just plain silly.

A cautious smile spread across his face, slowly

widening to a full grin. Suddenly she didn't care how she came across, just as long as he kept looking at her in that time-stopping manner.

"Sit," he commanded, and strolled around the counter to her supplies. He came up beside her and wiped her cheek with rubbing alcohol then lightly blew across her skin.

Each hair on her face, neck and chest stood on end as fine prickles formed on her skin. She tried not to sigh, choosing instead to sit perfectly still in the false guise of helping him out.

Rick ran his fingers through her ponytail, as if it was silken and precious. He traced the outline of her short bangs with his fingertip and followed along her hairline and around her ear.

She shuddered and exhaled, as though she'd forgotten to breathe for a long time.

Needing a modicum of control, she did her best and tried to sound nonchalant when she asked, "What are you doing back in town?"

"I live here," he said, appearing to be in deep concentration over color choice.

Trying to keep things light and bearable, she continued, "Did you know your father volunteered to work one of the booths?"

"I already dunked him. Twice." He'd dabbed a color or two on her skin, and stepped back to study his handiwork.

"You did?"

"Yeah, didn't you hear the cheers? Sweet."

She grinned. She could get used to the mesmerizing touch of Rick again.

He focused and meticulously painted her face for several seconds.

"There," he said, and stepped back. "No. Wait." He tickled her cheek yet again with a few finishing touches. "There."

He handed her the mirror and she almost dropped it when she saw what he'd written. She managed to read backwards in the mirror. "Will you marry me?" he'd written in bright rainbow colors.

He cocked a brow and waited.

Stunned, she stared first at the mirror and then into his intense brown eyes and almost came unglued.

Not an iota of insecurity could be detected on his face as he stood there before her, and everyone else in the park. His hands rested low on his denim-clad hips, and he waited for her to answer, as though it was the most logical question in the world to ask on a sunny Saturday afternoon. "Well?"

She gulped and grabbed his tickets. "Sit down."

He followed her lead. She forced her hands to get steady and picked up a brush. She dipped it into the red paint and wrote "Yes" across his forehead, then handed him the mirror.

His lips twitched into a smile, he planted his fingers around her arm and led her away from the booth. "Come with me," he said to her. And then over his shoulder he informed the other booth worker, "She's on a break."

Still trying to make her tongue and mouth work, China followed him. Fortunately, her legs were able to move, if not in uniform fashion.

In the distance, the jubilant sounds of people having

a great time could be heard. Another loud splash heralded that Dr. Morell had hit the water yet again. And China could have sworn she heard her mother's distinctive voice call out to him, "Bingo."

They walked on in silence until they reached a lone, out-of-the-way tree. Rick leaned against the trunk and drew China into his arms. Heat radiated from his chest to her palms through the thin cotton of his dark T-shirt. She looked into his face, the handsome man she'd missed with all of her heart since the night they'd made love. They stared at each other for a second before they kissed.

His lips lightly brushed hers, as though he only wanted a taste, but he couldn't resist more. His mouth covered hers and every sound in the park except for the loud beating of the pulse in her chest faded away.

God, she'd missed him.

She cupped his face, and felt early signs of stubble, and pressed her lips harder against his. She inhaled the fine spicy scent of his shower soap, felt his chest rise and fall, and heard a faint sound from his throat when he kissed her back.

China drifted away into the heaven of his warm, inviting kisses, and prayed this wasn't a dream. She tugged on his earlobes to make sure.

He pulled back. "What?"

She smiled. "Nothing." And immediately went back to kissing him. He co-operated wholeheartedly.

His hot hands stroked her arms, drawing her closer, before they came to rest on her hips. She settled her entire weight against him.

His mouth covered her ear. "You look beautiful today."

No words could have sent a deeper thrill through her than those. She'd quit hiding and he still found her beautiful. She nuzzled her head under his chin and sighed.

"I love you," she said proudly. "I'd have flown to Washington state to tell you. I promised myself to go after you, no matter what, once today's fair was over. But you beat me to it." She smiled, but soon grew serious. "I was scared and insecure that night at my apartment, and I said horrible things to you. Please, forgive me."

He tightened his arms around her, found her mouth and kissed her more deeply. "I do."

One of the fire trucks sounded its siren, startling them both, ending their special moment.

"Your straight talk gave me the incentive to finally stand up to my dad. I give you the credit for us talking civilly to each other for the first time in years."

Rick gently pulled her back into his embrace, and he caressed her face and looked deeply into her eyes. "I guess we both said some things the other needed to hear."

She nodded, wondering if it was possible to feel even more relief.

"Are you sure you want to marry the new Mercy Hospital ER supervisor?"

She smiled. "You got the job?"

He grinned at her. "I found out on Wednesday, the day I saw you. That's where I was headed when I couldn't stick around. Seems they had a change of heart, or rather my father did, and not because a certain Cass Seabury told him to." He smiled at her "Because he realized I deserved it. Somehow we managed to finally look at each other honestly without all our hang-ups clouding our judgement. We're going to try and start over. Anyway, they're going to announce it next week. So what do you say?"

"That depends," she said, feeling coy.

"Cruel. You need a pre-nup or something?"

"No. But are you sure you want to marry me with all my scars, inside and out?" She lifted a leg for his examination. "Even with legs like these?"

"Not in spite of your legs do I want to marry you, China. Because of them."

China moved out of Rick's embrace and tilted her head. "What do you mean?"

"You are who you are because of that accident, China. You've grown into an amazing, crusading, loving woman, and I want to share the rest of my life with you, and I gotta know now if you'll be my wife."

"My marrying the new ER supervisor depends on whether or not the ER supervisor will consider marrying the new Mercy Hospital public relations representative."

A slow grin spread across Rick's face. His dark eyes sparkled.

"You did great today, China. You'll be perfect for that job. And under those circumstances the new ER supervisor says sign me up. I still want to marry you."

He had no idea how much his approval meant to her. She'd broken through her chains, spoken in public, and had done a fine job of it, too, if she said so herself. She'd hung out her secrets and emotional laundry to dry and won the guy, all in one day. Life was good.

"In that case," she said, and tapped his forehead with her finger, "yes." She kissed him gently on the lips. "Today was perfect."

"And you're perfect for me, China," Rick said, edging closer for another kiss. One hand swept across her bare leg where it came to rest. He pressed his lips to her cheek before he looked into her eyes.

"I love you exactly the way you are."

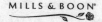

FREE!

4 Books
and a surprise gift!

We would like to take this opportunity to thank you for reading this Mills & Boon® book by offering you the chance to take FOUR more specially selected titles from the Medical Romance™ series absolutely FREE! We're also making this offer to introduce you to the benefits of the Mills & Boon® Reader Service™—

- ★ **FREE home delivery**
- ★ **FREE gifts and competitions**
- ★ **FREE monthly Newsletter**
- ★ **Exclusive Reader Service offers**
- ★ **Books available before they're in the shops**

Accepting these FREE books and gift places you under no obligation to buy, you may cancel at any time, even after receiving your free shipment. Simply complete your details below and return the entire page to the address below. You don't even need a stamp!

YES! Please send me 4 free Medical Romance books and a surprise gift. I understand that unless you hear from me, I will receive 6 superb new titles every month for just £2.89 each, postage and packing free. I am under no obligation to purchase any books and may cancel my subscription at any time. The free books and gift will be mine to keep in any case.

M7ZEF

Ms/Mrs/Miss/Mr ....Initials ....

BLOCK CAPITALS PLEASE

Surname ....

Address..

....

....Postcode ....

Send this whole page to:
UK: FREEPOST CN81, Croydon, CR9 3WZ